Praise for *Delirium*

'Lauren Oliver is the rising star of young adult fiction . . .
[*Delirium*] deftly conjures up a recognisably dystopian parallel
to our own world, as convincingly terrifying as the North
America of Margaret Atwood's *The Handmaid's Tale*.'
*The Sunday Times*

'Prepare to pull a sickie and be rooted to your chair with
one of the most addictive books we've come across in
ages . . . A recklessly romantic, smart, poignant and tense
read from one of the most exciting writers around . . .
Clever, moving and incredibly addictive.'
*Heat*

'A dystopian Romeo and Juliet story that deserves
to be as massive as *Twilight*.'
*Stylist*

Praise for *Pandemonium*

'Thrilling and thought-provoking . . . A thoughtful, exciting
and moving story that reminds us just how important love is.
Devour it, then go and give all your friends a big hug.'
*Heat*

'Prepare to become completely absorbed.'
*Glamour*

'We're big fans of Lauren Oliver and this is the emotionally
charged follow-up to last year's futuristic love story *Delirium* . . .
Now we just have to wait for the final episode in the trilogy.'
*Bella*

'Crackling with tension, Lauren Oliver's follow up to *Delirium* is
as whip smart and addictive as her dystopian debut.'
*Marie Claire*

Praise for *Requiem*

'It has been a long time since a book has had such an impact
on me . . . *Requiem* sucked me in from page one.'
*Glamour*

*Also by Lauren Oliver*

BEFORE I FALL

DELIRIUM
PANDEMONIUM
REQUIEM

THE BOOK OF SHHH
(AN ORIGINAL EBOOK)

PANIC

ROOMS

VANISHING GIRLS

*For younger readers*

LIESL & PO
THE SPINDLERS
CURIOSITY HOUSE: THE SHRUNKEN HEAD

# DELIRIUM
## STORIES
### HANA,
### ANNABEL, RAVEN
### & ALEX

# LAUREN OLIVER

First published in America in 2016 by HarperCollins Childrens Books
A division of HarperCollins Publishers

First published in Great Britain in 2016 by Hodder & Stoughton
An Hachette UK company

2

A CIP catalogue record for this title is available from the British Library

Paperback ISBN 978 1 473 63860 0
Ebook ISBN 978 1 473 63859 4

Typeset in Berkeley by Palimpsest Book Production Limited,
Falkirk, Stirlingshire

Printed and bound by Clays Ltd, St Ives plc

Hodder & Stoughton policy is to use papers that are natural,
renewable and recyclable products and made from wood grown in
sustainable forests. The logging and manufacturing processes are expected
to conform to the environmental regulations of the country of origin.

Hodder & Stoughton Ltd
Carmelite House
50 Victoria Embankment
London EC4Y 0DZ

www.hodder.co.uk

To all the fans of the Delirium trilogy:
Thank you for all your support, encouragement and
impassioned pleas about who Lena should choose.
You rock.

# Contents

# HANA

# one

**W**hen I was a little kid, my favorite thing about winter was sledding. Every time it snowed, I would convince Lena to meet me at the bottom of Coronet Hill, just west of Back Cove, and together we would trek through soft mounds of new powder, our breath coming in clouds, our plastic sleds sliding soundlessly behind us while hanging icicles refracted the sunlight and turned the world new and dazzling.

From the top of the hill, we could see all the way past the smudgy line of low brick buildings huddled together by the wharves and across the bay to the white-capped islands just off the coast – Little Diamond Island; Peaks Island, with its stiff-necked guard tower – past the massive patrol boats that trudged through the sleet-gray water on their way to other ports; all the way to open ocean, distant flashes of it winking and dancing close to the horizon.

'Today I'm going to go to China!' I'd trumpet out into the quiet.

And Lena would go as pale as the snow clinging to her faded jacket and say, 'Shhh, Hana. Someone will hear you.' We weren't supposed to talk about other countries, or even know their names. All these distant, diseased places were as good as lost to history – they had imploded, turned chaotic and riotous, ruined by *amor deliria nervosa*.

I had a secret map, though, which I kept underneath my mattress; it had been stuffed in with a few books I had inherited from my grandfather when he died. The regulators had gone through his possessions to make sure there was nothing forbidden among them, but they must have missed it: folded up and wedged inside a thick nursery-school primer, a beginner's guide to *The Book of Shhh,* was a map that must have been circulated in the time Before. It showed no border wall around the United States, and it featured other countries too: more countries than I had ever imagined, a vast world of damaged, broken places.

'China!' I would say, just to bug her, and to show her I wasn't afraid of being overheard, by the regulators or patrols or anyone else. Besides, we were all alone. We were always all alone at Coronet Hill. It was very steep, and situated close to the border and to Killians' House, which was supposedly haunted by the ghosts of a diseased couple who had been condemned to death for resistance during the blitz. There were other, more popular sledding spots all over Portland. 'Or maybe France. I hear France is lovely at this time of year.'

'*Hana.*'

'I'm just kidding, Lena,' I would say. 'I'd never go anywhere without you.' And then I'd flop down onto my sled and push off, just like that, feeling a fine spray of snow on my face as I gathered speed, feeling the frigid bite of the rushing air, watching the trees turn to dark blurs on either side of me. Behind me, I could hear Lena shouting, but her voice was whipped away by the thundering of the wind and the whistling of the sled across the snow and the loose, breathless laughter that pushed itself out of my chest. Faster, faster, faster, heart pounding and throat raw, terrified and exhilarated: a sheet of white, an endless surf of snow rising up to meet me as the hill began to bottom out . . .

Each time I made a wish: that I could take off into the air. I would be thrown from my sled and disappear into that bright, dazzling, blank tide, a crest of snow that would reach up and suction me into another world.

But each time, instead, the sled would begin to slow. It would come bumping and crunching to a halt, and I would stand up, shaking the ice from my mittens and from the collar of my jacket, and turn around to watch Lena take her turn – slower, more cautiously, letting her feet drag behind her to slow her momentum.

Strangely enough, this is what I dream about now, the summer before my cure, during the last summer that will ever be truly mine to enjoy. I dream about sledding. That's what it's like to barrel forward toward September, to speed toward the day when I will no longer be troubled by *amor deliria nervosa*.

It is like being on a sled in the middle of a cutting wind.

I am breathless and terrified; I will soon be engulfed by whiteness and suctioned into another world.

*Good-bye, Hana.*

'Perfect.' My mother dabs her mouth primly on her napkin and beams across the table at Mrs Hargrove. 'Absolutely exquisite.'

'Thank you,' Mrs Hargrove says, inclining her head graciously, as though she, and not her cook, has been the one to prepare the meal. My mom has a housekeeper who comes in three times a week, but I have never known a family with an actual staff. Mayor Hargrove and his family have real servants. They pass through the dining room, pouring water from sterling silver pitchers, refilling the bread plates, pouring out the wine.

'Didn't you think so, Hana?' My mother turns to me, widening her eyes so I can read the command in them.

'Absolutely perfect,' I reply obediently. My mother narrows her eyes at me slightly, and I can tell she's wondering whether I'm making fun of her. *Perfect* has been her favorite word this summer. Hana's performance at the evaluations was *perfect*. Hana's score was practically *perfect*. Hana was paired with Fred Hargrove – the mayor's son! Isn't that *perfect*? Especially since, well . . . There was that unfortunate situation with his first match . . . but everything always works out in the end . . .

'Mediocre at best,' Fred puts in casually.

Mayor Hargrove nearly chokes on his water. Mrs Hargrove gasps, 'Fred!'

Fred winks at me. I duck my head, hiding a smile.

'I'm kidding, Mom. It was delicious, as usual. But maybe Hana is tired of discussing the quality of the green beans?'

'Are you tired, Hana?' Mrs Hargrove has apparently not understood that her son is joking. She turns her watery gaze to me. Now Fred is concealing a smile.

'Not at all,' I say, trying to sound sincere. It is my first time having dinner with the Hargroves, and my parents have impressed on me for weeks how critical it is that they like me.

'Why don't you take Hana out to the gardens?' Mayor Hargrove suggests, pushing away from the table. 'It'll take a few minutes to get coffee and dessert on.'

'No, no.' The last thing I want is to be alone with Fred. He is nice enough, and thanks to the information packet I received about him from the evaluators, I'm well prepared to discuss his interests (golf; movies; politics), but nevertheless, he makes me nervous. He is older, and cured, and has already been matched once before. Everything about him – from the shiny silver cuff links to the neat way his hair curls around his collar – makes me feel like a little kid, stupid and inexperienced.

But Fred is already standing up. 'That's a great idea,' he says. He offers me his hand. 'Come on, Hana.'

I hesitate. It seems strange to have physical contact with a boy here, in a brightly lit room, with my parents watching me impassively – but of course, Fred Hargrove is my match, and so it is not forbidden. I take his hand, and he draws me up to my feet. His palms are very dry, and rougher than I expected.

We move out of the dining room and into a wood-paneled

hall. Fred gestures for me to go first, and I am uncomfortably aware of his eyes on my body, his closeness and smell. He is big. Tall. Taller than Steve Hilt.

As soon as I think of the comparison, I'm angry with myself.

When we step onto the back porch, I move away from him, and am relieved when he doesn't follow. I press up against the railing, staring out into the vast, dark-draped landscape of gardens. Small, scrolled-iron lamps illuminate birch trees and maples, trellises neat with climbing roses and beds of blood-red tulips. The crickets are singing, a throaty swell. The air smells like wet earth.

'It's beautiful,' I blurt.

Fred has settled onto the porch swing, keeping one leg crossed over the opposite knee. His face is mostly in shadow, but I can tell he's smiling. 'Mom likes gardening. Actually, I think she just likes weeding. I swear, sometimes I think she plants weeds just so she can yank them up again.'

I don't say anything. I've heard rumors that Mr and Mrs Hargrove have close ties to the president of *Deliria*-Free America, one of the most powerful anti-*deliria* groups in the country. It makes sense that she likes to weed, to uproot the nasty, creeping growth that blemishes her perfect garden. That is what the DFA wants too: total eradication of the disease, of the nasty, dark, twisting emotions that cannot be regulated or controlled.

I feel as though something hard and sharp is stuck in my throat. I swallow, reach out and squeeze the porch railing, taking comfort in its roughness and solidity.

I should be grateful. That's what my mother would tell me. Fred is good-looking, and rich, and he seems nice enough.

His father is the most powerful man in Portland, and Fred is being groomed to take his place. But the tightness in my chest and throat won't go away.

He dresses like his father.

My mind flashes to Steve – his easy laugh, his long, tan fingers skating up my thigh – and I will the image away quickly.

'I don't bite, you know,' Fred says lightly. I'm not sure whether he means it to be an invitation to move closer, but I stay where I am.

'I don't know you,' I say. 'And I'm not used to talking to boys.' This is no longer exactly true – not since Angelica and I discovered the underground, anyway – but of course, he can't know that.

He spreads his hands. 'I'm an open book. What do you want to know?'

I look away from him. I have many questions: *What did you like to do before you were cured? Do you have a favorite time of day? What was your first match like, and what went wrong?* But none are appropriate to ask. And he wouldn't answer me anyway, or he would answer the way he has been taught.

When Fred realizes I'm not going to speak, he sighs and climbs to his feet. 'You, on the other hand, are a complete mystery. You're very pretty. You must be smart. You like to run, and you were president of the debate team.' He has crossed the porch toward me, and he leans against the railing. 'That's all I got.'

'That's all there is,' I say forcefully. That hard thing in my throat is only growing. Although the sun went down an hour ago, it is still very hot. I find myself wondering, randomly, what Lena is doing tonight. She must be at home – it's nearly curfew. Probably reading a book, or playing a game with Grace.

'Smart, pretty, and simple,' Fred says. He smiles. 'Perfect.'

*Perfect.* There's the word again: a locked-door word – stifling, strangling.

I'm distracted by movement in the garden. One of the shadows is *moving* – and then, before I can cry out or alert Fred, a man emerges from the trees, carrying a large, military-style rifle. Then I do cry out, instinctively; Fred turns around and begins to laugh.

'Don't worry,' he says. 'That's just Derek.' When I continue to stare, he explains, 'One of Dad's guards. We've beefed up security recently. There have been rumors . . .' He trails off.

'Rumors about what?' I prompt him.

He avoids looking at me. 'It's probably overblown,' he says casually. 'But some people believe that a resistance movement is growing. Not everyone believes that the Invalids' – he winces when he says the word, as though it hurts him – 'were eradicated during the blitz.'

*Resistance movement. Invalids.* A prickly feeling starts to work its way through my body, as though I've just been plugged into an electrical outlet.

'My father doesn't believe it, of course,' Fred finishes flatly. 'Still, better to be safe than sorry, right?'

Once again, I stay quiet. I wonder what Fred would do if he knew about the underground, and knew that I had spent the summer at forbidden, unsegregated beach parties and concerts. I wonder what he would do if he knew that only last week, I let a boy kiss me, let him explore my thighs with his fingertips – actions reviled and forbidden.

'Would you like to go down into the gardens?' Fred asks, as though sensing the topic has disturbed me.

'No,' I say, so quickly and firmly he looks surprised. I inhale and manage to smile. 'I mean – I have to use the bathroom.'

'I'll show you where it is,' Fred says.

'No, please.' I can't keep the urgency from my tone. I toss my hair over one shoulder, tell myself to get a grip and smile again, wider this time. 'Stay here. Enjoy the night. I can find it.'

'And self-sufficient, too,' Fred says with a laugh.

On the way to the bathroom, I hear the murmur of voices coming from the kitchen – some of the Hargroves' servants, I assume – and am about to keep walking when I hear Mrs Hargrove say the word *Tiddles* quite clearly. My heart seizes. They're talking about Lena's family. I inch closer to the kitchen door, which is partially open, certain at first that I've only imagined it.

But then my mother says, 'Well, we never wanted to make little Lena feel ashamed because of the rest of her family. One or two bad apples . . .'

'One or two bad apples can mean the whole tree is rotten,' Mrs Hargrove says primly.

I feel a hot flash of anger and alarm – they *are* talking about Lena. For a second I fantasize about kicking open the kitchen door, right into Mrs Hargrove's simpering face.

'She's a lovely girl, really,' my mother insists. 'She and Hana have been inseparable since they were little.'

'You're much more understanding than I am,' Mrs Hargrove says. She pronounces *understanding* as though she's really saying *idiotic*. 'I would never have allowed Fred to run around with someone whose family had been so . . . tainted. Blood tells, doesn't it?'

'The disease doesn't carry through the blood,' my mother says softly. I feel a wild urge to reach through the wood and hug her. 'That's an old idea.'

'Old ideas are often based in fact,' Mrs Hargrove responds stiffly. 'Besides, we simply don't know all the factors, do we? Certainly an early exposure—'

'Of course, of course,' my mother says quickly. I can tell that she's eager to mollify Mrs Hargrove. 'It's all very complicated, I admit. Harold and I just always tried to allow things to progress naturally. We felt that at some point the girls would simply drift apart. They're too different – not well matched at all. I'm actually surprised their friendship lasted as long as it did.' My mother pauses. I can feel my lungs working painfully in my chest, as though I've been plunged into icy water.

'But after all, it seems we were right,' my mother continues. 'The girls have barely spoken at all this summer. So you see, in the end, it all worked out.'

'Well, *that's* a relief.'

Before I can move or react, the kitchen door is opening, and I am caught frozen, standing directly in front of the door. My mother lets out a small cry, but Mrs Hargrove doesn't look either surprised or embarrassed.

'Hana!' she chirps, smiling at me. 'What *perfect* timing. We were just about to have dessert.'

Back at home, locked in my room, I can breathe normally for the first time all night.

I draw a chair up to my window. If I press my face nearly

to the glass, I can just make out Angelica Marston's house. Her window is dark. I feel a pulse of disappointment. I need to do something tonight. There's an itch under my skin, an electric, jumpy feeling. I need to get out, need to *move*.

I stand up, pace the room, pick up my phone from the bed. It's late – after eleven – but for a moment I consider calling Lena's house. We haven't spoken in exactly eight days, since the night she came to the party at Roaring Brook Farms. She must have been horrified by the music and the people: boys and girls, uncureds, together. She looked horrified. She looked at me like I was already diseased.

I open the phone, type in the first three digits of her number. Then I snap the phone shut again. I've left messages with her already – two or three, probably, and she has returned exactly none of my calls.

Besides, she's probably sleeping, and I'll no doubt wake up her aunt Carol, who will think something is wrong. And I can't tell Lena about Steve Hilt – I don't want to frighten her, and for all I know she would report me. I can't tell her about what I'm feeling now, either: that my life is slowly squeezing closed around me, as though I'm walking through a series of rooms that keep getting smaller. She'll tell me how lucky I should feel, how grateful I should be for my scores at evaluations.

I throw my phone on the bed. Almost immediately, it buzzes: a new text message has come in. My heart leaps. Only a few people have my number – only a few people even have cell phones. I grab the phone again, fumble it open. The itch in my blood makes my fingers shake.

I knew it. The message is from Angelica.

*Can't sleep. Weird nightmares – was on the corner of Washington and Oak, and fifteen rabbits were trying to get me to join a tea party. I can't wait to get cured!*

All our messages about the underground must be carefully coded, but this one is easy enough to decipher. We're meeting on the corner of Washington and Oak in fifteen minutes.

We're going to a party.

# two

To get to the Highlands I have to go off peninsula. I avoid taking St John, even though it will lead me directly to Congress. There was an outbreak of the *deliria* there five years ago – four families affected, four early cures imposed. Since then, the whole street has been tainted and is always targeted by regulators and patrols.

The itch under my skin has swollen to a steady, thrumming force, a need in my legs and arms and fingers. I can barely pedal fast enough. I have to force myself not to push it. I need to stay alert and pay attention, just in case there are regulators nearby. If I'm caught out after curfew, I'll have a lot of questions to answer, and this – my last summer as me, my last summer of freedom – will come abruptly to a halt. I'll be thrown into the labs by the end of the week.

Luckily, I reach the Highlands without incident. I slow down, squinting at the street signs as I pass, trying to decipher letters in the dark. The Highlands is a mess of different roads and cul-de-sacs, and I never remember all of them. I pass Brooks and Stevens; Tanglewild and Crestview Avenue, and then, confusingly, Crestview Circle. At least the moon is full and floats almost directly above me, leering. Tonight the man in the moon looks as though he's winking, or smirking: a moon with secrets.

Then I spot Oak. Even though I'm barely rolling along now, my heart is going so hard in my throat, I feel like it'll burst out through my mouth if I try and say a word. I've avoided thinking about Steve all night, but now, as I get closer, I can't help it. Maybe he'll be here tonight. Maybe, maybe, maybe. The idea – the thought of him – cascades into consciousness, into being. There is no repressing it.

As I climb off my bike, I instinctively fumble in my back pocket and feel for the note I've been carrying everywhere for the past two weeks, after I found it folded neatly on top of my beach bag.

> *I like your smile. I want to know you. Study session 2nite*
> *– earth sciences. You have Mr Roebling, right?*
> *—SH*

Steve and I had seen each other at some of the underground parties earlier in the summer, and once we almost talked after I bumped into him and splashed some soda on his shoe. And then, during the day, we began to pass each other: in the street, at Eastern Prom. He always lifted his eyes to mine and, just for a second, flashed me a smile. That day – the day of the note – I thought I saw him wink. But I was with Lena, and he was with friends in the boys' section of the beach. No way for him to come and speak with me. I still don't know how he managed to sneak the note into my bag; he must have waited until the beach was pretty much empty.

His message, too, was in code. The 'study session' was an invitation to a concert; 'earth sciences' meant that it would be held on one of the farms – Roebling Farm, to be exact.

That night we ditched the concert and walked out to the middle of an empty field, and lay side by side in the grass with our elbows touching, looking up at the stars. At one point, he traced a dandelion from my forehead to my chin, and I fought the desperate, nervous urge to giggle.

That was the night he kissed me.

My first kiss. A new kind of kiss, like the new kind of music still playing, softly, in the distance – wild and arrhythmic, desperate. Passionate.

Since then, I have managed to see him only twice, and both times were in public and we could do no more than nod at each other. It is worse, I think, than not seeing him at all. That, too, is an itch – the desire to see him, to kiss him again, to let him put his fingers in my hair – is a monstrous, constant, crawling feeling in my blood and bones.

It's worse than a disease. It's a poison.

And I like it.

If he is here tonight – *please let him be here tonight* – I'm going to kiss him again.

Angelica is waiting for me on the corner of Washington and Oak, as promised. She is standing in the shadow of a towering maple, and for a second, as she steps out of the darkness – dark hair, dark shadow-eyes – I imagine that she is Lena. But then the moonlight falls differently on her face, and Lena's image goes skittering away into a corner of my mind. Angelica's face is all sharp angles, especially her nose, which is just slightly too long and tilted upward. That's the reason, I think, I disliked her for so long – her nose makes it look as though she's always smelling something nasty.

But she understands me. She understands what it's like to feel penned in, and she understands the need to break out.

'You're late,' Angelica says, but she's smiling.

Tonight there is no music. As we cross the lawn toward the house, a stifled giggle disturbs the silence, followed by the sudden swell of conversation.

'Careful,' Angie says as we step onto the porch. 'Third stair's rotten.'

I dodge it, like she does. The wood of the porch is old, and it groans under our weight. All the windows are boarded up, and the faint outlines of a large red X are still visible, faded by weather and time: this house was once home to the disease. When we were little, we used to dare one another to walk through the Highlands, dare each other to stand for as long as possible with our hands on the doors of houses that had been condemned. The rumor was that the tortured spirits of people who had died from *amor deliria nervosa* still walked the streets and would strike you down with disease for trespassing.

'Nervous?' Angie asks, sensing me shiver.

'I'm fine,' I say, and push open the door before she can reach for it. I enter ahead of her.

For a second, as we pass into the hallway, there is a sudden stillness, a moment of tension, as everyone in the house freezes; then they see that it is okay, that we are not regulators or police, and the tension ebbs away again. There is no electricity, and the house is full of candles — set on plates, stuffed into empty Coke cans, placed directly on the ground — which transform the walls into flickering, dissolving patterns of light, and turn people into shadows. And they, the shadow-people, are everywhere: massed in corners and on the few remaining pieces of furniture in the otherwise empty rooms, pressed into hallways, reclining on the stairs. But it is surprisingly quiet.

Almost everyone, I see, has coupled off. Boys and girls, intertwined, holding hands and touching each other's hair and faces and laughing quietly, doing all the things that are forbidden in the real world.

A mouth of anxiety yawns open inside of me. I have never been to any party like this. I can practically *feel* the presence of disease: the crawling of the walls, the energy and tension — like the nesting of a thousand insects.

*He has to be here.*

'This way.' Angie has instinctively dropped her voice to a whisper. She draws me toward the back of the house, and from the way she navigates the rooms, even in the dim and changing light, I can tell that she has been here several times before. We move into the old kitchen. More candles here illuminate the outlines of bare cupboards, a stove and a dark fridge with its door missing and its shelves black with spotted mold. The room smells stale, like sweat and mildew. A table in the center of the room holds a few dusty bottles of alcohol, and several girls are standing awkwardly against one counter while across the room a group of boys is pretending not to notice them. Obviously they have never been to a party like this either and are unconsciously obeying the rules of segregation.

I scan the boys' faces, hoping that Steve will be among them. He isn't.

'Do you want something to drink?' Angelica asks.

'Water,' I say. My throat feels dry, and it's very hot in the house. I almost wish that I had never left home. I don't know what I should do now that I'm here, and there is nobody I want to talk to. Angie is already pouring herself something to drink, and I know that she will soon disappear into the darkness with a boy. She does not seem out of place or anxious at all, and for a second I feel a flash of fear for her.

'There is no water,' Angie says, passing me a glass. I take a sip of whatever she has poured me and make a face. It's sweet but has the dull, stinging aftertaste of gasoline.

'What is it?' I say.

'Who knows?' Angie giggles and takes a sip from her own glass. Maybe she is nervous. 'It'll help you loosen up.'

'I don't need to—' I start to say, but then I feel hands on my waist, and my mind goes still and blank, and I find myself turning without intending to.

'Hi,' Steve says to me.

In the second it takes me to process that he is here, and real, and speaking to me, he leans in and puts his mouth on mine. This is only the second time I've ever been kissed, and I have a momentary panic where I forget what I am supposed to do. I feel his tongue pressing into my mouth and I jerk, surprised, spilling a bit of my drink. He pulls away, laughing.

'Happy to see me?' he asks.

'Hi to you, too,' I say. I can still taste his tongue in my

mouth – he has been drinking something sour. I take another sip of my drink.

He leans in and puts his mouth right up to my ear. 'I was hoping you would come,' he says in a low voice. Warmth breaks across my chest.

'Really?' I say. He doesn't respond; he takes my hand and draws me out of the kitchen. I swivel around to tell Angelica I'll be back, but she has disappeared.

'Where are we going?' I ask, trying to sound unconcerned.

'It's a surprise,' he says.

The warmth from my chest has made it into my head now. We move through a vast room full of more shadow-people, more candles, more flickering shapes on the wall. I place my drink on the arm of a ratty sofa. A girl with short, spiky hair is curled there on the lap of a boy; he is nuzzling her neck and his face is concealed. But she glances up at me as I pass, and I am momentarily startled: I recognize her. She has an older sister at St Anne's, Rebecca Sterling, a girl I was kind-of friends with. I remember Rebecca told me that her younger sister had chosen to go to Edison because it was bigger.

Sarah. Sarah Sterling.

I doubt she recognizes me, but she drops her eyes quickly.

At the far end of the room is a rough wooden door. Steve leans into it and we emerge onto a porch even sadder than the one out front. Someone has placed a lantern out here – maybe Steve? – illuminating the yawning gaps between wood slats, places where the wood has rotted away completely.

'Careful,' he says as I nearly miss my footing and go plunging through a bad patch.

'I've got it,' I say, but am grateful that he tightens his grip on my hand. I tell myself that this is it – what I wanted, what I had hoped for tonight – but somehow the thought keeps skittering away. He grabs the lantern before we step off the porch and carries it, swinging, in his free hand.

Across an overgrown stretch of lawn, the grasses shin-high and covered with moisture, we reach a small gazebo, painted white and lined with benches. In places, wildflowers have begun to push their way up through the floorboards. Steve helps me into it – it is elevated a few feet above the ground, but if there were stairs at one point, they are gone now – and then follows me.

I test one of the benches. It seems sturdy enough, so I sit down. The crickets are singing, tremulous and steady, and the wind carries the smell of damp earth and flowers.

'It's beautiful,' I say.

Steve sits next to me. I'm uncomfortably aware of every part of our skin that is touching: knees, elbows, forearms. My heart starts beating hard, and once again I am having trouble breathing.

'You're beautiful,' he says. Before I can react, he finds my chin with his hand and tilts me toward him, and then we're kissing again. This time, I remember to kiss back, to move my mouth against his, and I am not so surprised when his tongue finds the inside of my mouth, although the feeling is still foreign and not totally pleasant. He is breathing hard, twisting his fingers through my hair, so I think he must be enjoying himself – I must be doing it correctly.

His fingers graze my thigh, and then, slowly, he lowers his hand, begins massaging my thigh, working up toward my hips. All my feeling, all my concentration, flows down to that spot and to the way my skin feels, as though it is burning in response to his touch. This has to be *deliria*. Doesn't it? This must be what love feels like, what everyone has warned me about. My mind is spinning uselessly, and I'm trying to remember the symptoms of *deliria* listed in *The Book of Shhh*, as Steve's hand moves higher and his breathing gets even more desperate. His tongue is so deep in my mouth, I'm worried I might choke.

Suddenly all I can think about is a line from the Book of Lamentations: *What glitters may not be gold; and even wolves may smile; and fools will be led by promises to their deaths.*

'Wait,' I say, pushing away from him.

'What's wrong?' Steve traces his finger from my cheekbone to my chin. His eyes are on my mouth.

*Preoccupation – difficulty concentrating.* A symptom comes back to me finally. 'Do you think about me?' I blurt. 'I mean, have you thought about me?'

'All the time.' His answer comes quickly, easily. This should make me happy but I feel more confused than ever. Somehow I always imagined that I would know if the disease was taking root – that I would feel it instinctively, a shift deep in my blood. But this is simply tension, and shredding anxiety, and the occasional burst of good feeling.

'Relax, Hana,' he says. He kisses my neck, moves his mouth to my ear, and I try to do as he says and let go of the warmth traveling from my chest to my stomach. But I can't stop the questions; they surge, pressing closely in the dark.

'What's going to happen to us?' I say.

He pulls away, sighing, and rubs his eyes. 'I don't know what you—' he begins, and then breaks off with a small exclamation. 'Holy shit! Look, Hana. Fireflies.'

I turn in the direction he is looking. For a moment, I see

nothing. Then all at once, several flares of white light burst in midair, one after another. As I watch, more and more of them float out of the blackness – brief sparks circling dizzyingly around one another, then sinking once again into the dark, a hypnotic pattern of illumination and extinguishment.

Out of nowhere, I feel a strong surge of hope, and I find myself laughing. I reach for his hand and tighten my fingers around his. 'Maybe it's a sign,' I say.

'Maybe,' he says, and leans in to kiss me again, and so my question – *What's going to happen to us?* – goes unanswered.

# three

I wake to blinding sunshine and a searing pain in my head; I forgot to draw the shades last night. There's a sour taste in my mouth. I move clumsily to the bathroom, brush my teeth and splash water on my face. As I straighten up, I see it: a blue-purple blemish on my neck just below my right ear, a tiny constellation of bruised and broken capillaries.

I don't believe it. He gave me a Devil's Kiss.

We always got checked for kisses at school; we had to stand in a line with our hair pulled back while Mrs Brinn examined our chests, necks, collarbones, shoulders. Devil's Kisses are a sign of illegal activity – and a symptom, too, of the disease taking root, spreading through your bloodstream. Last year, when Willow Marks was caught in Deering Oaks

Park with an uncured boy, the story was that she'd been under surveillance for weeks, after her mom had noticed a Devil's Kiss on her shoulder. Willow was taken out of school to get cured a full eight months before her scheduled procedure, and I haven't seen her since.

I rummage through the bathroom cabinet, and luckily manage to find an old tube of foundation and some yellowish concealer. I layer on the makeup until the kiss is no more than a faint blue spot on my skin, then arrange my hair in a messy side-bun knotted just behind my right ear. I'll have to be very careful over the next few days; I'm sporting a mark of the disease. The idea is both thrilling and terrifying.

My parents are downstairs in the kitchen. My father is watching the morning news. Even though it's Sunday, he is dressed for work and eating a bowl of cereal standing up. My mother is on the telephone, working its cord around her finger, making the occasional noise of assent. I know immediately that she must be talking to Minnie Phillips. My father watches the news; my mother calls Minnie for information. Mrs Phillips works at the records bureau, and her husband is a policeman – between the two of them, they know everything that happens in Portland.

*Almost* everything, that is.

I think of the twisting, darkened rooms of uncureds last night – all of them touching, whispering, breathing one another's air – and feel a rush of pride.

'Morning, Hana,' my dad says without taking his eyes off the television screen.

'Good morning.' I'm careful to keep the left side of my body angled toward him as I slide into a chair at the kitchen table and shake a handful of cereal into my palm.

Donald Seigal, the mayor's minister of information, is being interviewed on TV.

'Stories of a resistance are vastly overblown,' he is saying smoothly. 'Still, the mayor is responsive to the concerns of the community . . . new measures will be effectuated . . .'

'Unbelievable.' My mother has hung up the phone. She takes the remote and mutes the television. My father makes a noise of irritation. 'Do you know what Minnie just told me?'

I fight the urge to smile. I knew it. That is the thing about people once they're cured: they're predictable. That is, supposedly, one of the procedure's benefits.

My mom continues, without waiting for a response, 'There was *another* incident. A fourteen-year-old girl this time, and a boy from CPHS. They were caught sneaking around the streets at three in the morning.'

'Who was it?' my dad asks. He has given up on the news and is now rinsing his bowl in the sink.

'One of the Sterling girls. The younger one, Sarah.' My mother watches my dad expectantly. When he doesn't react, she says, 'You remember Colin Sterling and his wife. We had lunch with them at the Spitalnys' in March.'

My father grunts.

'So terrible for the fam—' My mother stops abruptly, turning to me. 'Are you all right, Hana?'

'I – I think I swallowed the wrong way,' I gasp. I stand up and reach for a glass of water. My fingers are shaking.

Sarah Sterling. She must have been caught on her way back from the party, and for a second I have the worst, most selfish thought: *thank God it wasn't me*. I take long, slow sips of water, willing my heart to stop pounding. I want to ask what happened to Sarah – what *will* happen – but I don't trust myself to speak. Besides, these stories always end the same way.

'She'll be cured, of course,' my mother finishes, as though reading my mind.

'She's too young,' I blurt out. 'There's no way it'll work right.'

My mother turns to me calmly. 'If you're old enough to catch the disease, you're old enough to be cured,' she says.

My father laughs. 'Soon you'll be volunteering for the DFA. Why not operate on infants, too?'

'Why not?' My mother shrugs.

I stand up, bracing myself against the kitchen table as a rush of blackness sweeps through my head, clouding my vision. My father takes the remote and turns the volume up on the television again. Now it is Fred's father, Mayor Hargrove, whose image comes into focus.

'I repeat, there is no danger of a so-called "resistance movement", or any significant spread of the disease,' he is saying. I walk quickly out into the hall. My mom calls something to me, but I'm too focused on the drone of Hargrove's voice – 'Now, as ever, we declare a zero-tolerance policy for disruptions and dissidence' – to hear what she says. I take the stairs two at a time and shut myself into my room, wishing more than ever that my door had a lock.

But privacy breeds secrecy, and secrecy breeds sickness.

My palms are sweating as I pull out my phone and dial Angelica's number. I'm desperate to talk to someone about what happened to Sarah Sterling – I need Angelica to tell me it's okay, and we're safe, and also that the underground won't be disrupted – but we'll have to speak carefully, in

codes. All our phone calls are regulated and recorded, periodically, by the city.

Angelica's cell phone goes straight to voice mail. I dial her
house number, which rings and rings. I have a flash of panic:
for a second, I worry she must have been caught too. Maybe
even now, she's being dragged down to the labs, strapped
down for her procedure.

But no. She lives a few doors down from me. If Angelica
had been caught, I would have heard about it.

The urge is there, sudden and overwhelming: I need to
see Lena. I need to talk with her, to spill everything, to tell
her about Fred Hargrove, who has already had and given up
one match, and his mother's obsessive weeding, and Steve
Hilt, and the Devil's Kiss, and Sarah Sterling. She will make
me feel better. She will know what I should do – what I
should *feel*.

This time, when I go downstairs, I make sure to tiptoe; I
don't want to have to answer my parents' questions about
where I'm heading. I get my bike from the garage, where I
stashed it after riding home last night. A purple scrunchie
is looped around its left handle. Lena and I have the same
bike, and a few months ago we started using the scrunchies
to differentiate them. After our fight I pulled the scrunchie
off and shoved it in the bottom of my sock drawer. But the
handlebars looked sad and naked, and so I had to replace
it.

It is just after eleven, and the air is full of shimmering,
wet heat. Even the seagulls seem to be moving more slowly;
they drift across the cloudless sky, practically motionless, as
though they are suspended in liquid blue. Once I make it
out of the West End and its protective shelter of ancient oaks

and shaded, narrow streets, the sun is practically unbearable, high and unforgiving, as though a vast glass lens has been centered over Portland.

I make a point of detouring past the Governor, the old statue that stands in the middle of a cobblestone square near the University of Portland, which Lena will attend in the fall. We used to run together past the Governor regularly, and made a habit of reaching up and slapping his outstretched hand. I always made a wish simultaneously, and now, although I don't stop to slap his hand, I reach out with a toe and skim the base of the statue for good luck as I ride past. *I wish,* I think, but don't get any further. I don't know exactly what to wish for: to be safe or to be unsafe, for things to change or for things to stay the same.

The ride to Lena's house takes me longer than usual. A garbage truck has broken down on Congress Street, and the police are redirecting people up Chestnut and around on Cumberland. By the time I get to Lena's street, I'm sweating, and I stop when I'm still a few blocks away from her house to drink from a water fountain and blot my face. Next to the fountain is a bus stop, with a sign warning of curfew restrictions – SUNDAY TO THURSDAY, 9 P.M.; SATURDAY AND SUNDAY, 9:30 P.M. – and as I go to chain my bike up, I notice the smudgy glass waiting area is papered with flyers. They are all identical, and feature the crest of Portland above bolded black type.

*The Safety of One Is the Duty of All*
*Keep Your Eyes and Ears Open*
*Report All Suspicious Activity to the Department of*
*Sanitation and Security*

*If You See Something, Say Something*
**$500 reward for reports of illicit or unapproved activity*

I stand for a minute, scanning the words over and over, as though they will suddenly mean something different. People have always reported suspicious behavior, of course, but it has never come with a financial reward. This will make it harder, much harder, for me, for Steve, for all of us. Five hundred dollars is a lot of money to most people these days – the kind of money most people don't make in a week.

A door slams and I jump, almost knocking over my bike. I notice, for the first time, that the whole *street* is papered with flyers. They are posted on gates and mailboxes, taped to disabled streetlamps and metal garbage cans.

There is movement on Lena's porch. Suddenly she appears, wearing an oversized T-shirt from her uncle's deli. She must be going to work. She pauses, scanning the street – I think her eyes land on me, and I lift my hand in a hesitant wave, but her eyes keep tracking, drifting over my head, and then sweeping off in the other direction.

I'm about to call out to her when her cousin Grace comes flying down the cement porch steps. Lena laughs and reaches out to slow Grace down. Lena looks happy, untroubled. I'm seized by sudden doubt: it occurs to me that Lena might not miss me at all. Maybe she hasn't been thinking of me; maybe she's perfectly happy not speaking to me.

After all, it's not like she's tried to call.

As Lena starts making her way down the street, with Grace bobbing beside her, I turn around quickly and remount my bike. Now I'm desperate to get out of here. I don't want her to spot me. The wind kicks up, rustling all those flyers, the exhortations of safety. The flyers lift and sigh in unison, like a thousand people waving white handkerchiefs, a thousand people waving good-bye.

# four

The flyers are just the beginning. I notice that there are more regulators on the streets than usual, and there are rumors – neither confirmed nor denied by Mrs Hargrove, who comes over to deliver a scarf that my mother left – that there will soon be a raid. Mayor Hargrove is insistent – both on television and when we once again dine with his family, this time at their golf club – that there is no resurgence of the disease and no reason to worry. But the regulators, and the offers of rewards, and the rumors of a possible raid, tell a different story.

For days there is not even a whisper of another underground gathering. Every morning I rub concealer into the Devil's Kiss on my neck, until at last it disperses and breaks apart, leaving me both relieved and saddened. I haven't seen

Steve Hilt anywhere – not at the beach, not at Back Cove or by the Old Port – and Angelica has been distant and guarded, although she manages to slip me a note explaining that her parents have been watching her more closely since the news of Sarah Sterling's exposure to *deliria*.

Fred takes me golfing. I don't play, so instead I trail behind him on the course as he shoots a near-perfect game. He is charming and courteous and does a semi-decent job of pretending to be interested in what I have to say. People turn to look at us as we pass. Everyone knows Fred. The men greet him heartily, ask after his father, congratulate him on getting paired, although no one breathes a word about his first wife. The women stare at me with frank and unconcealed resentment.

I am lucky.

I am suffocating.

The regulators crowd the streets.

Lena still doesn't call.

Then one hot evening at the end of July, there she is: she barrels past me on the street, her eyes trained deliberately on the pavement, and I have to call her name three times before she will turn around. She stops a little way up the hill, her face blank – unreadable – and makes no effort to come toward me. I have to jog uphill to her.

'So what?' I say as I get closer, panting a little. 'You're just going to walk by me now?' I meant for the question to come out as a joke, but instead it sounds like an accusation.

She frowns. 'I didn't see you,' she says.

I want to believe her. I look away, biting my lip. I feel like I could burst into tears – right there in the shimmering, late-afternoon heat, with the city spread out like a mirage beyond Munjoy Hill. I want to ask her where she's been, and tell her I miss her, and say that I need her help.

But instead what comes out is: 'Why didn't you call me back?'

She blurts out at the same time: 'I got my matches.'

I'm momentarily taken aback. I can't believe that after days of abrupt and unexplained silence, this is what she would say to me first. I swallow back all the things I was going to say to her and make my tone polite, disinterested.

'Did you accept yet?' I say.

'You called?' she says. Again, we both speak at the same time.

She seems genuinely surprised. On the other hand, Lena has always been hard to read. Most of her thoughts, most of her true feelings, are buried deep.

'I left you, like, three messages,' I say, watching her face closely.

'I never got any messages,' Lena says quickly. I don't know whether she is telling the truth. Lena, after all, always insisted that after the cure we wouldn't be friends – our lives would be too different, our social circles too remote. Maybe she has decided that already the differences between us are too great.

I flash back to how she looked at me at the party at Roaring Brook Farms – the way she jerked away when I tried to reach out to her, lips curling back. Suddenly I feel as though I am only dreaming. I am dreaming of a too-colored, too-vivid day, while images pass soundlessly in front of me – Lena is moving her mouth, two men are loading buckets into a truck, a little girl wearing a too-big swimsuit is scowling at us from a doorway – and I am speaking too, responding, even smiling, while my words are sucked into silence, into the bright white light of a sun-drenched dream. Then we are walking. I am walking with her toward her house, except I am only drifting, floating, skating above the pavement.

Lena speaks; I answer. The words are only drifting too – they are a nonsense-language, a dream-babble.

Tonight I will attend another party in Deering Highlands with Angelica. Steve will be there. The coast is once again clear. Lena looks at me, repulsed and fearful, when I tell her this.

It doesn't matter. None of it matters anymore. We are sledding once again – into whiteness, into a blanket of quiet.

But I am going to keep going. I am going to soar, and soar, and break away – up, up, up into the thundering noise and the wind, like a bird being sucked into the sky.

We pause at the beginning of her block, where I stood just the other day, watching her move happily and unself-consciously down the sidewalk with Grace. The flyers still paper the street, although today there is no wind. They hang perfectly, corners aligned, the emblazoned governmental seal running like a typographical error hundreds of times along the two sides of the street. Lena's other cousin, Jenny, is playing soccer with some kids at the end of the block.

I hang back. I don't want to be spotted. Jenny knows me, and she's smart. She'll ask me why I don't come around anymore, she'll stare at me with her hard, laughing eyes, and she'll know – she'll *sense* – that Lena and I are no longer friends, that Hana Tate is evaporating, like water in the noon sun.

'You know where to find me,' Lena is saying, gesturing casually down the street. *You know where to find me.* Like that, I am dismissed. And suddenly I no longer feel as though I am dreaming, or floating. A dead weight fills me, dragging me back into reality, back into the sun and the smell of garbage and the shrill cries of the kids playing soccer in the street, and Lena's face, composed, neutral, as though she has already been cured, as though we have never meant a thing to each other in our lives.

The weight is rising through my chest, and I know that at any second, I'm going to begin crying.

'Okay, then. See you around,' I say quickly, concealing the break in my voice with a cough and a wave. I turn around and start walking quickly, as the world begins to spiral together into a wash of color, like liquid being spun down a drain. I jam my sunglasses down onto my nose.

'Okay. See you,' Lena says.

The tide is pushing from my chest to my throat now, carrying with it the urge to turn around and call out to her, to tell her I miss her. My mouth is full of the sour taste that rises up with those old, deep words, and I can feel the muscles in my throat flexing, trying to press them back and down. But the urge becomes unbearable, and without intending to, I find that I am spinning around, calling her name.

She has already made it back to her house. She pauses with her hand on the gate. She doesn't say a word; she just stares at me blankly, as though in the time it has taken her to walk the twenty feet, she has already forgotten who I am.

'Never mind,' I call out, and this time when I turn around, I do not hesitate or look back.

The note from Steve arrived earlier this morning inside a rolled-up advertisement for *Underground Pizza – Grand Opening TONIGHT!*, which had been wedged into one of the narrow iron scrolls on our front gate. The note was only three words – *Please be there* – and included only his initials, presumably so in case it had been discovered by my parents or a regulator instead, neither of us would be implicated. On the back of the advertisement was a crudely drawn map showing only a single street name: Tanglewild Lane, also in Deering Highlands.

This time, there is no need to sneak out. My parents have gone to a fund-raiser tonight; the Portland Conservation Society is having their annual dinner-dance. Angelica's parents are attending too. This makes things far easier. Rather than sneak through the streets after curfew, Angelica and I meet in the Highlands early. She has brought a half bottle of wine and some bread and cheese, and she is red-faced and excited. We sit on the porch of a now-shuttered mansion and eat our dinner while the sun breaks into waves of red and pink beyond the tree line, and finally ebbs away altogether.

Then, at half past nine, we make our way toward Tangle-wild.

Neither of us has the exact address, but it doesn't take us long to locate the house. Tanglewild is only a two-block street, mostly wooded, with a few peaked roofs rising up – just barely visible, silhouetted against the deepening purple sky – indicating houses set back behind the trees. The night is remarkably still, and it is easy to pick out the drumbeat thrumming underneath the noise of the crickets. We turn down a long, narrow drive, its pavement full of fissures, which the moss and the grass have begun to colonize. Angelica takes her hair down, then places it in a ponytail, then once again shakes it loose. I feel a deep flash of pity for her, followed by a squeeze of fear.

Angelica's cure is scheduled for next week.

As we get close to the house, the rhythm of the drum gets

louder, although it is still muffled; all the windows have been boarded up, I notice, and the door is closed tightly and stuffed around with insulation. The second we open the door, the music becomes a roar: a rush of banging and screeching guitar, vibrating through the floorboards and walls. For a second I stand, disoriented, blinking in the bright kitchen light. The music seems to get my head in a vise – it squeezes, it presses out all other thoughts.

'I said, close the *door*.' Someone – a girl with flame-red hair – launches past us practically shouting, and slams the door behind us, keeping the sound in. She shoots me a dirty look as she goes back across the kitchen to the guy she has been talking to, who is tall and blond and skinny, all elbows and kneecaps. Young. Fourteen at most. His T-shirt reads portland naval conservatory.

I think of Sarah Sterling and feel a spasm of nausea. I close my eyes and concentrate on the music, feeling it vibrate up through the floor and into my bones. My heart adjusts to its rhythm, beating hard and fast in my chest. Until recently I had never heard music like this, only the stately, measured songs that get played endlessly on Radio One. This is one of my favorite things about the underground: the crashing of the cymbals, the screeching guitar riffs, music that moves into the blood and makes you feel hot and wild and alive.

'Let's go downstairs,' Angelica says. 'I want to be closer to the music.' She's scanning the crowd, obviously looking for someone. I wonder if it's the same someone she went off with at the last party. It's amazing that despite all the things we've shared this summer, there's still so much that we don't and can't talk about.

I think of Lena and our strained conversation in the street.

The now-familiar ache grips my throat. If only she had listened to me and tried to understand. If she could see the beauty of this underground world, and appreciate what it means: the music, the dancing, the feeling of fingertips and lips, like a moment of flight after a lifetime of crawling . . .

I push the thought of Lena away.

The stairs leading down to the basement are rough-hewn concrete. Except for a few thick pillar candles, pooled in wax and placed directly on the steps, they are swallowed in dark. As we descend, the music swells to a roar, and the air becomes hot and sticky with vibration, as though the sound is gaining physical shape, an invisible body pulsing, breathing, sweating.

The basement is unfinished. It looks as though it was hacked straight out of the earth. It's so dark I can just make out rough stone walls and a stone ceiling, spotted with dark mold. I don't know how the band can see what they are playing.

Maybe that's the reason for the screeching, careening notes, which seem to be fighting with one another for dominance – melodies competing and clashing and clawing into the upper registers.

The basement is vast and cavelike. A central room, where the band is playing, branches into other, smaller spaces, each one darker than the last. One room is nearly blocked off with heaps of broken furniture; another one is dominated by a sagging sofa and several dirty-looking mattresses. On one of them a couple is lying, writhing against each other. In the dark, they look like two thick snakes, intertwined, and I back away quickly. The next room is crisscrossed with laundry lines; from them, dozens of bras and pairs of cotton underwear – girls' underwear – are hanging. For a second, I think they must have been left by the family who lived there, but as a group of boys pushes roughly past me, snickering loudly, it occurs to me all at once that these must be trophies, mementos, of things that have happened in this basement.

*Sex.* A word that is difficult even to think.

I feel dizzy and hot already. I turn around and see that Angelica has once again melted into the darkness. The music is driving so fiercely through my head, I'm worried it will split apart. I start to move back to the central room, thinking that I will go upstairs, when I spot Steve standing in the corner, his eyes half-closed, his face lit up red by a small cluster of miniature lights that are coiled on the ground and connected, somehow, to a circuit – probably the same one that is powering the amps in the central room.

As I start toward him, he spots me. For a second, his face registers no change of expression. Then I step closer, into the limited circle of dim light, and he grins. He says something, but his face is swallowed by a crescendo of sound as the two guitar players bang furiously on their instruments.

We both step forward simultaneously, closing the last few feet between us. He loops his arms around my waist, and his fingers brush the exposed skin between my shirt and waistband, thrilling and hot. I go to rest my head against his chest at the same time as he bends down to kiss me, so he ends up planting his lips on my forehead. Then, as I tilt my face upward and he stoops to try again, I crack my head against his nose. He jerks back, wincing, bringing a hand to his face.

'Oh my God. I'm so sorry.' The music is so loud, I can't even hear my own apology. My face is flaming. But when he draws his hand away from his nose, he's smiling. This time, he bends down slowly, with exaggerated care, making a joke of it – he kisses me cautiously, slides his tongue gently between my lips. I can feel the music vibrating in the few inches between our chests, beating my heart into a frenzy. My body is full of such rushing heat, I'm worried it will go fluid – I'll melt; I'll collapse into him.

His hands massage my waist and then move up my back, pulling me closer. I feel the sharp stab of his belt buckle against my stomach, and inhale sharply. He bites down lightly on my lip – I'm not sure if it's an accident. I can't think, can't breathe. It's too hot, too loud; we're too close. I try to pull away but he's too strong. His arms tighten around me, keeping me pressed to his body, and his hands skate down my back again, over the pockets of my shorts, find my bare legs. His fingers trace my inner thighs, and my mind flashes to that room of crisscrossed underwear, all of it hanging limply in the dark, like deflated balloons, like the morning-after detritus of a birthday party.

'Wait.' I place both hands on his chest and shove him forcibly away. He is red-faced and sweating. His bangs are plastered against his forehead. 'Wait,' I say again. 'I need to talk to you.'

I'm not sure if he hears me. The rhythm of the music is still drumming beneath my ribs, and my words are just another vibration skating alongside of it. He says something – again, indecipherable – and I have to lean forward to hear him better.

'I said, I want to dance!' he yells. His lips bump against my ear, and I feel the soft nibble of his teeth again. I jerk away quickly, then feel guilty. I nod and smile to show him *okay*, we can dance.

Dancing, too, is new for me. Uncureds are not allowed to

dance in couples, although Lena and I used to practice sometimes with each other, mimicking the stately, grave way we'd
seen married couples and cureds dance at official events:
stepping evenly in time with the music, keeping at least an
arm's distance between their chests, rigid and strict. *One*
two-three, *one* two-three, Lena would bellow, as I would
practically choke from laughing so hard, and she'd nudge
me with a knee to keep me on track, and assume the voice
of our principal, McIntosh, telling me that I was a *disgrace,
an absolute disgrace.*

The kind of dancing I have known is all about rules:
patterns, holds and complicated maneuvers. But as Steve
draws me closer to the band, all I can see is a frenzied mass
of seething, writhing people, like a many-headed sea snake,
grinding, waving their arms, stamping their feet, jumping.
No rules, just energy – so much energy, you could harness
it; I bet you could power Portland for a decade. It is more
than a wave. It's a tide, an ocean of bodies.

I let myself break apart on it. I forget about Lena, and
Fred Hargrove, and the posters plastered all around Portland.
I let the music drill through my teeth and drip out my hair
and pound through my eyeballs. I taste it, like grit and sweat.
I am shouting without meaning to. There are hands on my
body – Steve's? – gripping me, pulsing the rhythm into my
skin, traveling the places no one has ever touched – and
each touch is like another pulse of darkness, beating softness
into my brain, beating rational thoughts into a deep fog.

Is this freedom? Is it happiness? I don't know. I don't care
anymore. It is different – it is being alive.

Time becomes a stutter – the space between drumbeats,
splintered into fragments, and also endlessly long, as long as

soaring guitar notes that melt into one another, as full as the dark mass of bodies around me. I feel like the air downstairs has gone to liquid, to sweat and smell and sound, and I have broken apart in it. I am wave: I am pulled into the everything. I am energy and noise and a heartbeat going *boom, boom, boom*, echoing the drums. And although Steve is next to me, and then behind me, drawing me into him, kissing my neck and exploring my stomach with his fingers, I can hardly feel him.

And for a moment – for a split second – everything else falls away, the whole pattern and order of my life, and a huge joy crests in my chest. I am no one, and I owe nothing to anybody, and my life is my own.

Then Steve is pulling me away from the band and leading me into one of the smaller rooms branching off from it. The first room, the room with the mattresses and the couch, is packed. My body still feels only distantly attached, clumsy, as though I am a puppet unused to walking on its own. I stumble against a couple kissing in the dark. The girl whips around to face me.

Angelica. My eyes go instinctively to the person she was kissing, and for a second time freezes, and then jump-cuts forward. I feel a seesawing in my stomach, like I've just watched the world flip upside down.

Another girl. Angelica is kissing another girl.

Angelica is an Unnatural.

The look on Angelica's face passes from irritation to fear to fury.

'Get the hell out of here,' she practically snarls. Before I can say anything, before I can even say it's okay, she reaches out and shoves me backward. I stumble against Steve. He steadies me, leans down to whisper in my ear.

'You okay there, princess? Too many drinks?'

Obviously, he has not seen. Or maybe he has – he doesn't know Angelica; it wouldn't matter to him. It doesn't matter to me, either – it's the first time I've ever really thought about it, but the idea is there, immediate and absolute – it doesn't matter to me one tiny shred.

*Chemicals gone wrong. Neurons misfiring, brain chemistry warped.* That's what we were always taught. All problems that would be obliterated by the cure. But here, in this dark, hot space, the question of chemicals and neurons seems absurd and irrelevant. There is only what you want and what happens. There is only grabbing on and holding tight in the darkness.

I immediately regret what I must have looked like to Angelica: shocked, maybe even disgusted. I'm tempted to go back and find her, but Steve has already pulled me into another small room, this one empty except for the heaping pile of broken furniture, which over time has been split apart and vandalized. Before I can speak, he presses me against the wall and starts kissing me. I can feel the sweat on his chest, seeping through his T-shirt. He starts hitching up my shirt.

'Wait.' I manage to wrench my mouth away from his.

He doesn't respond. He finds my mouth again and slides his hands toward my rib cage. I try to relax, but all that pops into my head is an image of the laundry lines heavy with bras and underwear.

'Wait,' I say again. This time I sidestep him and manage to put space between us. The music is muffled here, and we'll be able to talk. 'I need to ask you something.'

'Anything you want.' His eyes are still on my lips. It's distracting me. I edge away from him even farther.

My tongue suddenly feels too big for my mouth. 'Do you

– do you like me?' At the last second, I can't bring myself to ask what I really want to know: *Do you love me? Is this what love feels like?*

He laughs. 'Of course I like you, Hana.' He reaches out to touch my face, but I pull away an inch. Then, maybe realizing the conversation won't be quick, he sighs and runs a hand through his hair. 'What's this about, anyway?'

'I'm scared,' I blurt. Only when I say it do I realize how true it is: fear is strangling me, suffocating me. I don't know what's more terrifying: the fact that I will be found out, that I will be forced to go back to my normal life, or the possibility that I won't. 'I want to know what's going to happen to us.'

Abruptly, Steve gets very still. 'What do you mean?' he asks cautiously. There has been a short gap between songs; now the music starts up again in the next room, frenzied and discordant.

'I mean how can we . . .' I swallow. 'I mean, I'm going to be cured in the fall.'

'Right.' He's looking at me sideways, suspiciously, as though I'm speaking another language and he can identify only a few words at a time. 'So am I.'

'But then we won't . . .' I trail off. My throat is knotting up. 'Don't you want to be with me?' I ask finally.

At that, he softens. He steps toward me again, and before I have a chance to relax, he has woven his hands in my hair. 'Of course I want to be with you,' he says, leaning down to whisper the words in my ear. He smells like musky aftershave and sweat.

It takes a huge effort for me to push him away. 'I don't mean here,' I say. 'I don't mean like this.'

He sighs again and steps away from me. I can tell I've

started to annoy him. 'What's the problem here?' he asks. His voice is hard-edged, vaguely bored. 'Why can't you just relax?'

That's when it hits me. It is as though my insides have been vacuumed away and all that remains is a solid rock of certainty: he doesn't love me. He doesn't care about me at all. This has been nothing but fun for him: a forbidden game, like a child trying to steal cookies before dinner. Maybe he was hoping I'd let him shimmy me out of my underwear. Maybe he was planning to clip my bra alongside all the others, a sign of his secret triumph.

I've been fooling myself this whole time.

'Don't be upset.' Steve must sense that he's made the wrong move. His voice turns soft again, lilting. He reaches for me again. 'You're so pretty.'

'Don't touch me.' I jerk backward and accidentally knock my head against the wall. Starbursts explode in my vision.

Steve puts a hand on my shoulder. 'Oh, shit, Hana. Are you okay?'

'I said, don't touch me.' I push roughly past him, careening into the next room, which is now so packed with people I can barely force my way toward the stairs. I hear Steve call my name only once. After that, he either gives up or his voice is drowned in the coursing swell of sound. It is hot; everyone is slick with sweat, lost in shadow, as though they've been floundering in oil. Even when my vision clears, I feel unsteady on my feet.

I need air.

I need to get out of here. There's a roaring in my head, distinct from the throb of the music – a distant, high-pitched scream knifing me in two.

I stop moving. No. The scream is real. Someone is screaming. For a second I think I must have imagined it – it must have been the music, which continues screeching on – but then all at once the scream crests and becomes a huge surge, coasting over the sound of the band.

'Run! Raid! Run!'

I am frozen, paralyzed with fear. The music breaks off with a crash. Now there is nothing but screaming, and I am being pushed, shoved by the waves of people around me.

'Raid! Run!'

Out. Out. I need to get out. Someone elbows me in the back, and I barely manage to right myself. Stairs – I need to get to the stairs. I can see them from where I am standing, can see a surge of people fighting and clawing upward. Then suddenly there is a tremendous splinter of wood and a crest in the screaming. The door at the top of the stairs has been shattered; the people behind it are falling, tumbling into the people behind them, who are tumbling, tumbling down . . .

This isn't happening. It can't be.

A man is silhouetted huge in the great, gaping mouth of the shattered door. A regulator. He is holding a gun. From behind him, two giant shapes rocket forward into the crowd, and the screams swell in pitch and become the sounds of snarling and snapping.

Dogs.

As the regulators start forcing their way in, my body at last unfreezes. I turn around, away from the stairs, into the thick mass of people, all shoving and running in different directions: openmouthed, panicked. I'm hemmed in on all sides. By the time I force myself out of the main room, several regulators have made it down the stairs. I glance behind them and see them scything through the crowd with their nightsticks.

A huge, amplified voice is booming, 'This is a raid. Do not try to run. Do not try to resist.'

There is a small ground-level window set high in the room with the dingy mattresses and the couch, and people are crowded around it, yelling at one another, fumbling for a latch or a way to open it. A boy springs onto the sofa and swings hard at the window with his elbow. It shatters outward. He stands on the arm of the sofa and hoists himself up and through it. Now people are fighting to get out this way. People are swinging at one another, clawing, fighting to be first.

I look over my shoulder. The regulators are drawing closer, their heads bobbing above the rest of the crowd, like grim-faced sailors pushing through a storm. I'll never make it out in time.

I struggle against the current of bodies, which is flowing strong toward the window, to the promise of escape, and hurtle into the next room. This is where I stood with Steve and asked him whether he liked me only five minutes ago, although it already seems like the dream from a different lifetime. There are no windows here, no doors or exits.

Hide. It's the only thing to do. Hide and hope that there are too many people to sniff out one by one. I pick my way quickly around the enormous pile of debris heaped against one wall, over broken-down chairs and tables and old strips of tattered upholstery.

'This way, this way!'

The regulator's voice is loud enough, close enough, to be heard over the chaos of other sounds. I stumble, catching my shin against a piece of rusted metal. The pain is sharp and makes my eyes water. I ease down into the space between the wall and the pile of junk and slowly adjust the metal sheet so that it blocks me from view.

Then there is nothing to do but wait, and listen, and pray.

Every minute is an hour and an agony. I wish, more than anything, that I could put my hands over my ears and hum, drown out the terrible soundtrack that's looping around me: the screaming, the thud of the nightsticks, the dogs snarling and barking. And the people begging, too, pleading as they are hauled away in handcuffs: *Please, you don't understand, please, let me go, it was a mistake, I didn't mean to* . . . Over and over again, a nightmare-song stuck on repeat.

Suddenly I think of Lena, lying safe somewhere in her bed, and my throat squeezes up and I know I'm going to cry. I've been so stupid. She was right about everything. This isn't a game. It wasn't worth it either – the hot, sweaty nights, letting Steve kiss me, dancing – it has all amounted to nothing. Meaningless.

The only meaning that matters is the dogs and the regulators and the guns. That is the truth. Crouching, hiding, pain in my neck and back and shoulders. That is reality.

I squeeze my eyes shut. *I'm sorry, Lena. You were right.* I imagine her giving a fitful stir in her sleep, kicking one heel out of the blanket. The thought gives me some comfort. At least she's safe, away from here.

Hours: time is elastic, gaping like a mouth, squeezing me down a long, narrow, dark throat. Even though the basement must be ninety degrees, I can't stop shivering. As the sounds of the raid begin to quiet, finally, I'm worried that the chattering of my teeth will give me away. I have no idea what time it is or how long I've been crouched against the wall.

I can no longer feel the pain in my back and shoulders; my whole body feels weightless, outside my control.

At last it is silent. I edge cautiously out from my hiding place, hardly daring to breathe. But there is no movement anywhere. The regulators have gone, and they must have caught or chased out everyone who was here. The darkness is impermeable, a stifling blanket. I still don't want to risk the stairs, but now that I am free, and moving, the need to get *out*, to escape this house, is rising like panic inside me. A scream is pressing at my throat, and the effort of swallowing back makes my throat hurt.

I feel my way toward the room with the couch. The window high in the wall is just visible; beyond it, the sheen of dew on the grass glows slightly in the moonlight. My arms are shaking. I can barely manage to haul myself up onto the ledge, scooting forward with my face in the dirt, inhaling the smell of growth, still fighting the urge to scream, or sob.

And then, finally, I'm out. The sky glitters with hard-edged stars, vast and indifferent. The moon is high and round, lighting the trees silver.

There are bodies lying in the grass.

I run.

# five

The morning after the raids, I wake up to a message from Lena.

'*Hana, you need to call me. I'm working today. You can reach me at the store.*'

I listen to it twice, and then a third time, trying to judge her tone. Her voice has none of its usual singsong, no teasing lilt. I can't tell whether she's angry or upset or just irritated.

I am dressed and on my way to the Stop-N-Save before realizing I've made the decision to see her. I still feel as though a great block of ice has been lodged inside me, in my very center, making me feel numb and clumsy. Somehow, miraculously, I managed to sleep when I at last made it home, but my dreams were full of screams, and dogs drooling blood.

Stupid: that is what I've been. A child, a fairy-tale chaser.

Lena was right all along. I flash to Steve's face – bored, detached, waiting for me to finish my tantrum – to his silken voice, like an unwanted touch: *Don't be upset. You're so pretty.*

A line from *The Book of Shhh* comes back to me: *There is no love, only disorder.*

I've had my eyes closed all this time. Lena was right. Lena will understand – she'll have to, even if she's still angry at me.

I slow my bike as I pedal past Lena's uncle's storefront, where Lena works shifts all through the summer. I don't spot anyone but Jed, though, a huge lump of a man who can barely string a sentence together to ask you whether you'd like to buy a Big Gulp soda for a dollar. Lena always thought he must have been damaged by the cure. Maybe she's right. Or maybe he was just born that way.

I pull around to the narrow alley in back, which is crowded with Dumpsters and smells sickly sweet, like old, rotten trash. A blue door halfway down the alley marks the entrance to the storeroom in the back of the Stop-N-Save. I can't think of how many times I've come here to hang with Lena while she's supposed to be doing inventory, snacking on a stolen bag of chips and listening to a portable radio I snagged from my parents' kitchen. For a moment, I get a fierce ache underneath my ribs, and I wish I could go back – vacuum over this summer and the underground parties and Angelica. There were so many years when I didn't think about *amor deliria nervosa* at all, or question *The Book of Shhh* or my parents.

And I was happy.

I prop my bike against a Dumpster and knock softly on the door. Almost immediately, it scrapes inward.

Lena freezes when she sees me. Her mouth falls open a

little. I've been thinking about what I wanted to say to her all morning, but now – confronted by her shock – the words shrivel up. She was the one who told me to find her at the store, and now she's acting like she's never seen me before.

What comes out is, 'Are you going to let me in, or what?'

She starts, as though I've just interrupted a daydream. 'Oh, sorry. Yeah, come in.' I can tell she's just as nervous as I am. There's a jumpy, hopped-up energy to her movements. When I enter the storeroom, she practically slams the door behind me.

'Hot in here.' I'm biding time, trying to shake loose all the words I planned on saying. *I was wrong. Forgive me. You were right about everything.* They're coiled like wires in the back of my throat, electric-hot, and I can't get them to unwind. Lena says nothing. I pace the room, not wanting to look at her, worried that I'll see the same expression I saw on Steve's face last night – impatience, or worse, detachment. 'Remember when I used to come and hang out with you here? I'd bring magazines and that stupid old radio I used to have? And you'd steal—'

'Chips and soda from the cooler,' she finishes. 'Yeah, I remember.'

Silence stretches uncomfortably between us. I continue circling the small space, looking everywhere but at her. All those coiled words are flexing and tightening their metal fingers, shredding at my throat. Unconsciously, I've brought my thumb to my mouth. I feel small sparks of pain as I begin ripping at the cuticles, and it brings back an old comfort.

'Hana?' Lena says softly. 'Are you okay?'

That single stupid question breaks me. All the metal fingers relax at once, and the tears they've been holding back come surging up at once. Suddenly I am sobbing and telling her everything: about the raid, and the dogs, and the sounds of skulls cracking underneath the regulators' nightsticks. Thinking about it again makes me feel like I might puke. At a certain point, Lena puts her arms around me and starts murmuring things into my hair. I don't even know what she's saying, and I don't care. Just having her here – solid, real, on my side – makes me feel better than I have in weeks. Slowly I manage to stop crying, swallowing back the hiccups and sobs that are still running through me. I try to tell her that I've missed her, and that I've been stupid and wrong, but my voice is muffled and thick.

Then somebody knocks on the door, very clearly, four times. I pull away from Lena quickly.

'What's that?' I say, dragging my forearm across my eyes, trying to get control of myself. Lena tries to pass it off as though she hasn't heard. Her face has gone white, her eyes wide and terrified. When the knocking starts up again, she doesn't move, just stays frozen where she is.

'I thought nobody comes in this way.' I cross my arms, watching Lena narrowly. There's a suspicion needling, pricking at some corner of my mind, but I can't quite focus on it.

'They don't. I mean – sometimes – I mean, the delivery guys—'

As she stammers excuses, the door opens, and *he* pokes his head in – the boy from the day Lena and I jumped the gate at the lab complex, just after we had our evaluations. His eyes land on me and he, too, freezes.

At first I think there must be a mistake. He must have knocked on the wrong door. Lena will yell at him now, tell him to clear off. But then my mind grinds slowly into gear and I realize that no, he has just called Lena's name. This was obviously planned.

'You're late,' Lena says. My heart squeezes up like a shutter, and for just a second the world goes totally dark. I have been wrong about everything and everyone.

'Come inside and shut the door,' I say sharply. The room feels much smaller once he is in it. I've gotten used to boys this summer but never here, like this, in a familiar place and in daylight. It is like discovering that someone else has been using your toothbrush; I feel both dirty and disoriented. I feel myself swivel toward Lena. 'Lena Ella Haloway Tiddle.' I pronounce her full name, very slowly, partly because I need to reassure myself of her existence – Lena, my friend, the worried one, the one who always pleaded for safety first, who now makes secret appointments to meet with boys. 'You have some explaining to do.'

'Hana, you remember Alex,' Lena says weakly, as though that – the fact of my remembering him – explains anything.

'Oh, I *remember* Alex,' I say. 'What I don't remember is why Alex is *here*.'

Lena makes a few unconvincing noises of excuse. Her eyes fly to his. A message passes between them. I can *feel* it, encoded and indecipherable, like a zip of electricity, as though I've just passed too close to one of the border fences. My stomach turns. Lena and I used to be able to speak like that.

'Tell her,' Alex says softly. It is as though I'm not even in the room.

When Lena turns to me, her eyes are pleading. 'I didn't mean to' is how she starts. And then, after a second's pause, she spills. She tells me about seeing Alex at the party at Roaring Brook Farms (*the party I invited her to; she wouldn't have been there if it wasn't for me*), and meeting him down by Back Cove just before sunset.

'That's when – that's when he told me the truth. That he was an *Invalid*,' she says, keeping her eyes locked on mine and forcing out the word, *Invalid*, in a normal volume. I unconsciously suck in a breath. So it's true; all this time, while the government denied and denied, there have been people living on the fringes of our cities, uncured and uncontrolled.

'I came to find you last night,' Lena says more quietly. 'When I knew there was going to be a raid . . . I snuck out. I was there when – when the regulators came. I barely made it out. Alex helped me. We hid in a shed until they were gone . . .'

I close my eyes and reopen them. I remember wiggling into the damp earth, bumping my hip against the window. I remember standing, and seeing the dark forms of bodies lying like shadows in the grass, and the sharp geometry of a small shed, nestled in the trees.

Lena was there. It is almost unimaginable.

'I can't believe that. I can't believe you snuck out during a raid – for me.' My throat feels thick again, and I will myself not to start crying. For a moment I am overwhelmed by a feeling so huge and strange, I have no name for it: it surges over the guilt and the shock and the envy; it plunges a hand into the deepest part of myself and roots me to Lena.

For the first time in a long time, I actually *look* at her. I've always thought Lena was pretty, but now it occurs to me that at some point – last summer? last year? – she became beautiful. Her eyes seem to have grown even larger, and her cheekbones have sharpened. Her lips, on the other hand, look softer and fuller.

I've never felt ugly next to Lena, but suddenly I do. I feel tall and ugly and bony, like a straw-colored horse.

Lena starts to say something when there's a loud knock on the door that opens into the store, and Jed calls out, 'Lena? Are you in there?'

Instinctively I shove Alex sideways so he stumbles behind the door just as it begins to open from the other side. Fortunately, Jed manages to get it open only a few inches before the door collides with a large crate of applesauce. I wonder, fleetingly, whether Lena placed it there for that purpose.

Behind me, I can *feel* Alex: he is both very alert and very still, like an animal just before bolting. The door muffles the sound of Jed's voice. Lena keeps a smile on her face when she replies to him. I can't believe this is the same Lena who used to hyperventilate when she was asked to read in front of the class.

My stomach starts twisting, knotted up with conflicting admiration and resentment. All this time, I thought we were growing apart because I was leaving Lena behind. But really it was the reverse. She was learning to lie.

She was learning to love.

I can't stand to be so close to this boy, this Invalid, who is now Lena's secret. My skin is itching.

I pop my head around the door. 'Hi, Jed,' I say brightly. Lena gives me a grateful look. 'I just came by to give Lena something. And we started gossiping.'

'We have customers,' Jed says dully, keeping his eyes locked on Lena.

'I'll be out in a second,' she says. When Jed withdraws again with a grunt, closing the door, Alex lets out a long breath. Jed's interruption has restored tension to the room. I can feel it crawling along my skin, like heat.

Perhaps sensing the tension, Alex kneels down and begins unpacking his backpack. 'I brought some things for your leg,' he says quietly. He has brought medical supplies. When Lena rolls up one leg of her jeans to her knee, she reveals an ugly wound on the back of her calf. I feel a quick, swinging sense of vertigo and a surge of nausea.

'Damn, Lena,' I say, trying to keep my voice light. I don't want to freak her out. 'That dog got you good.'

'She'll be fine,' Alex says dismissively, as though I shouldn't worry about it – as though it's none of my concern. I have the sudden urge to kick him in the back of his head. He is kneeling in front of Lena, dabbing antibacterial cream on her leg. I'm mesmerized by the way his fingers move confidently along her skin, as though her body is his to treat and touch and tend to. *She was mine before she was yours*: the words are there, unexpectedly, surging from my throat to my tongue. I swallow them back.

'Maybe you should go to the hospital.' I direct the words to Lena, but Alex jumps in.

'And tell them what? That she got hurt during a raid on an underground party?'

I know he's right, but that doesn't stop me from feeling an irrational swell of resentment. I don't like the way he's acting as though he's the only one who knows what's good for Lena. I don't like the way she's looking at him like she agrees.

'It doesn't hurt that bad.' Lena's voice is gentle, mollifying, the voice of a parent soothing a stubborn child. Once again I have the sense that I am seeing her for the first time: she is like a figure behind a scrim, all silhouette and blur, and I barely recognize her. I can't stand to look at her anymore – Lena, a stranger – so I drop to my knees and practically elbow Alex out of the way.

'You're doing it wrong,' I say. 'Let me.'

'Yes, ma'am.' He shuffles out of the way without protest, but he stays crouched down, watching me work. I hope he won't notice that my hands are shaking.

Out of nowhere, Lena starts laughing. I'm so surprised, I almost drop the gauze right as I'm in the middle of tying it off. When I look up at Lena, she's laughing so hard, she has to double forward and put a hand over her mouth to try to muffle the sound. Alex watches her soundlessly for a minute – he's probably just as shocked as I am – and then he, too, lets out a snort of laughter. Soon they're both cracking up.

Then I start laughing too. The absurdity of the situation hits me all at once: I came here to apologize, to tell Lena she has been right to be cautious and keep safe, and instead I surprised her with a boy. No, even worse – an Invalid. After all this time and despite all her warnings, Lena is the one who has caught the *deliria*; Lena is the one with the biggest secrets – shy Lena, who has never even liked to stand up in front of the class, has been sneaking around and breaking every rule we have been taught. The laughter comes in spasms. I laugh until my stomach aches and tears are streaming down my cheeks. I laugh until I can't even tell if I'm laughing or whether I've started crying again.

What will I remember about the summer when it is over?

Twin feelings of pleasure and pain: oppressive heat, the frigid bite of the ocean, so cold it lodges in your ribs and takes your breath away; eating ice cream so fast a headache rises from the teeth to the eyeballs; endless, boring evenings with the Hargroves, stuffing myself with food better than any I have ever eaten in my life; and sitting with Lena and Alex at 37 Brooks in the Highlands, watching a beautiful sunset bleed out into the sky, knowing that we are one day closer to our cures.

Lena and Alex.

I have Lena back again, but she is changed, and it seems that every day she grows a little more different, a little more distant, as though I am watching her walk down a darkening hallway. Even when we are alone – which is rare now; Alex is almost always with us – there is a vagueness to her, as though she is floating through her life in the middle of a daydream. And when we are with Alex, I might as well not be there. They speak in a language of whispers and giggles and secrets; their words are like a fairy-tale tangle of thorns, which place a wall between us.

I am happy for her. I am.

And sometimes, just before going to sleep, when I am at my most vulnerable, I am jealous.

What else will I remember, if I remember anything at all?

The first time Fred Hargrove kisses my cheek, his lips are dry on my skin.

Racing with Lena to the buoys at Back Cove; the way she smiled when she confessed she'd done the same thing with Alex; and discovering when we got back to the beach that my soda had turned warm, syrupy, undrinkable.

Seeing Angelica, post-cure, helping her mother clip roses in their front yard; the way she smiled and waved cheerfully, her eyes unfocused, as though they were fixated on some imaginary spot above my head.

Not seeing Steve Hilt at all.

And rumors, persistent rumors: of Invalids, of resistance, of the growth of the disease, spreading its blackness among us. Every day, streets papered with more and more flyers. *Reward, reward, reward.*

*Reward for information.*

*If you see something, say something.*

A paper town, a paper world: paper rustling in the wind, whispering to me, hissing out a message of poison and jealousy.

*If you know something, do something.*

I'm sorry, Lena.

# ANNABEL

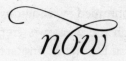

*now*

When I was a girl, it snowed for a whole summer. Every day, the sun rose smudgy behind a smoke-gray sky and hovered behind its haze; in the evenings, it sank, orange and defeated, like the glowing embers of a dying flame.

And the flakes came down and down – not cold to touch, but with their own peculiar sting – as the wind brought smells of burning.

Every night, my mother and father sat us down to watch the news. All the pictures were the same: towns neatly evacuated, cities enclosed, grateful citizens waving from the windows of big, shiny buses as they were carted off to a new future, a life of perfect happiness. A life of painlessness.

'See?' my mother would say, smiling at me and my sister,

Carol, in turn. 'We live in the greatest country on earth. See how lucky we are?'

And yet the ash continued swirling down, and the smells of death came through the windows, crept under the door, hung in our carpets and curtains, and screamed of her lie.

Is it possible to tell the truth in a society of lies? Or must you always, of necessity, become a liar?

And if you lie to a liar, is the sin somehow negated or reversed?

These are the kinds of questions I ask myself now: in these dark, watery hours, when night and day are interchangeable. No. Not true. During the day the guards come, to deliver food and take the bucket; and at night the others moan and scream. They are the lucky ones. They are the ones who still believe that sound, that voice, will do any good. The rest of us know better, and have learned to live in silence.

I wonder what Lena is doing now. I always wonder what Lena is doing. Rachel, too: both my girls, my beautiful, big-eyed girls. But I worry about Rachel less. Rachel was always harder than Lena, somehow. More defiant, more stubborn, less *feeling*. Even as a girl, she frightened me – fierce and fiery-eyed, with a temper like my father's once was.

But Lena . . . little darling Lena, with her tangle of dark hair and her flushed, chubby cheeks. She used to rescue spiders from the pavement to keep them from getting squashed; quiet, thoughtful Lena, with the sweetest lisp to break your heart. To break my heart: my wild, uncured, erratic, incomprehensible heart. I wonder whether her front teeth still overlap; whether she still confuses the words *pretzel* and *pencil* occasionally; whether the wispy brown hair grew straight and long, or began to curl.

I wonder whether she believes the lies they told her.

I, too, am a liar now. I've become one, of necessity. I lie when I smile and return an empty tray. I lie when I ask for *The Book of Shhh,* pretending to have repented.

I lie just by being here, on my cot, in the dark.

Soon, it will be over. Soon, I will escape.

And then the lies will end.

# then

The first time I saw Rachel and Lena's father I knew: knew I would marry him, knew I would fall in love with him. Knew he would never love me back, and I wouldn't care.

Picture me: seventeen, skinny, scared. Wearing a too-big, beat-up denim jacket I'd bought from a thrift store and a hand-knitted scarf, not even close to warm enough to immunize me from the frigid December wind, which came howling across the Charles River, blew the snow sideways, stripped people in the streets of all their color so they walked, white as ghosts, heads bowed against the fury.

That was the night Misha took me to see the cousin of a friend of a friend, Rawls, who ran a Brain Shop down on Ninth.

That's what we called the dingy centers that sprang up in the decade after the cure became law: Brain Shops. Some of them pretended to be at least half-legit, with waiting rooms like at a regular doctor's office and tables for lying down. In others, it was just some guy with a knife, ready to take your money and give you a scar, hopefully one that looked realistic enough.

Rawls's shop was the second kind. A low basement room, painted black for God knows what reason; a sagging leather couch, a small TV, a stiff-backed wooden chair, and a space heater – and that was pretty much it, except for the smell of blood, a few buckets and a little curtained-off area, too, where he actually did his work.

I remember I nearly threw up coming in, I was so nervous. A couple of kids were ahead of me. There was no space on the couch, and I had to stand. I kept thinking the walls were contracting; I was terrified they would collapse entirely, burying us there.

I'd run away from home almost a month earlier and in that time had been scraping and saving money for a fake.

In those days it was easier to travel; a decade after the cure was perfected, the walls were still going up, and regulations weren't as stringent. Still, I'd never been more than twenty miles from home, and I spent practically the whole bus ride down to Boston either with my nose pressed up against the window, watching the bleak blur of starved winter trees and shivering landscapes and guard towers, new and in construction – or in the bathroom, sick with nerves, trying to hold my breath against the sharp stink of pee.

The last commercial flight: that's what I watched on TV, at Rawls's shop, while I waited my turn. The news crews packing the runway, the roar of the plane down the strip, and then the lift: an impossible lift, like a bird's, so beautiful and easy it made you want to cry. I'd never been on an airplane, and now I never would. The airstrips would be dismantled and airports abandoned. Too little gas, too much risk of contagion.

I remember my heart was in my throat, and I couldn't look away from the TV, from the image of the plane as it morphed, grew smaller, turned into a small black bird against the clouds.

That's when they came: soldiers, young recruits, fresh out of boot camp. Uniforms crisp and new, boots shining like oil. People were trying to run out the exit in the back, and everyone was shouting. The curtains got torn down; I saw a flimsy folding table covered by a sheet, and a girl stretched out on it, bleeding from her neck. Rawls must have been halfway through her procedure.

I wanted to help her, but there wasn't any time.

The back door was thrown open, and I made it out and into an alley slick with ice, heaped with dirty snow and trash. I fell, cut my hand on the ice, kept going. I knew if I was caught, that was the end – I'd be hauled back to my parents, chucked into the labs, probably ranked a zero.

That was the first year that a national system of ranking was established, made consistent across the country. Pairing was taking off. Regulatory councils were springing up everywhere, and little kids talked about becoming evaluators when they grew up.

And no one would choose the girl with the record.

It was at the corner of Linden and Adams that I saw him. Ran into him, actually – saw him step out in front of me, hands up, shouting, 'Wait!' Tried to dodge, lost my footing, stumbled directly into his arms. I was so close, I could see the snow caught in his lashes, smell the damp wool of his coat and the sharpness of aftershave, see where he'd missed the stubble on his jaw. So close that the procedural scar on his neck looked like a tiny white starburst.

I'd never been that close to a boy before.

The soldiers behind me were still shouting – 'Stop!' and 'Hold her!' and 'Don't let her get away!' I'll never forget the way he looked at me – curiously, almost amused, as though I were a strange species of animal in a zoo.

Then: he let me go.

*now*

The dagger pin is all I have left. It is comfort and pain, both, because it reminds me of all I've had, held and had taken from me.

It is my pen, too. With it, I write my story, again and again, in the walls. So I don't forget. So it becomes real.

I think of: Conrad's hands; Rachel's dark hair; Lena's rosebud mouth; how, when she was an infant, I used to sneak into her bedroom and hold her while she slept. Rachel never let me – from birth, she screamed, kicked, would have woken the household and the street.

But Lena lay still and warm in my arms, submerged in some secret dreamland.

And she was my secret: those nighttime hours, that twin heartbeat space, the darkness, the joy.

All of this, I write.

And so truth shall set me free.

My room is full of holes. Holes where the stone grows porous, eaten away by mold and moisture. Holes where the mice make their homes. Holes of memory, where people and things get lost.

There is a hole in the bottom of my mattress.

And in the wall behind my bed, another hole, growing bigger by the day.

On the fourth Friday of every month, Thomas brings me a change of linens for the cot. Laundry day is my favorite. It helps me keep track of the days. And for the first few nights, before the new sheet is soiled with sweat and the sediment of dust that sifts down on me continuously, like snow, I feel almost human again. I can close my eyes, imagine I am back in the warmth of the old house, with the wood and the sun, the smell of detergent, an illegal song piping softly from the ancient record player.

And, of course, laundry day is when I get my messages.

Today I'm up just before the sun. My cell is windowless, and for years I couldn't tell night from day, morning from evening: a colorless existence, a time without aging or end. In the first year of my imprisonment, I did nothing but dream of the outdoors – the sun on Lena's hair, warm wooden steps, the smell of the beach at low tide, swollen-belly rain clouds.

Over time even my dreams became gray and textureless.

Those were the years I wanted to die.

When I first broke through the wall, after three years of digging, twisting, carving the soft stone away with a bit of metal no larger than a child's finger – when that last bit of rock crumbled away and went spinning, tumbling into the river below – my first thought wasn't even of escape but of air, sun, breath. I slept for two nights on the floor just so I could feel the wind, so I could inhale the smell of snow.

Today I have stripped my cot of its single sheet and the coarse blanket – wool in winter, cotton in summer – that is standard issue in Ward Six. No pillows. I once heard the warden say that a prisoner had tried to suffocate himself here, and ever since, pillows have been forbidden. It seems unlikely but then again: two years ago a prisoner managed to get hold of a guard's broken shoelaces and choked himself to death on the metal frame of his cot.

I am at the end of the row, so as always, I get to listen to the rest of the ritual: the doors creaking open, the occasional cry or moan, the squeak of Thomas's sneakers and then the heavy thud, the click, of the cell doors closing again. This is my only excitement, my only pleasure: waiting for the clean linens, holding the filthy sheet balled in my lap, heart fluttering like a moth in my throat, thinking, *Maybe, maybe this time . . .*

Amazing, how hope lives. Without air or water, with hardly anything at all to nurture it.

The bolts slide back. A second later, the door grinds open and Thomas appears, carrying a folded sheet. I haven't seen my reflection in eleven years – since I arrived and sat in the medical wing while a female warden cut off my hair and shaved my head with a razor, telling me it was for my own good – so the lice would stay out.

My monthly shower takes place in a windowless, mirrorless room, a stone box with several rusted showerheads and no hot water, and now when my head needs shaving, the warden comes to me, and I am bound and locked to a heavy metal ring on the door while she works. It is by watching Thomas, by seeing the way the years have made his skin puff and sag, carved wrinkles into the corners of his eyes, thinned his hair, that I can estimate what they have done to me.

He passes me the new sheet and removes my soiled one. He says nothing. He never does, not out loud. It's too risky. But for a second, his eyes meet mine, and some communication passes between us.

Then it's over. He turns and leaves. The door shuts and the bolt clicks into place.

I stand and move to the cot. My hands are shaking as I unfold the sheet. Inside it is a pillowcase, carefully concealed, no doubt smuggled up from one of the other wards.

Time is really just a test of patience. This is how it works, how it has worked for years: a pillowcase one month, occasionally an extra sheet. Linens that go missing and aren't looked for, linens that can be torn, twisted, braided together.

I reach into the pillowcase. At the very bottom is a small piece of paper, also carefully folded, containing Thomas's sole instructions: *Not yet*.

My disappointment is physical: a bitter rush of taste, a liquid feeling in my stomach. Another month to wait. I know I should be relieved – the rope I've been making is still too short, and will leave me with a ten-foot drop to the Presumpscot River. More chances to slip, twist or break something, cry out.

And I absolutely cannot cry out.

To keep from thinking too much about the wait ahead of me, another thirty days in this airless, dark place – another thirty days closer to death – I get down on my hands and knees and maneuver under the cot, feeling for the hole in the mattress, as big as a fist. Over the course of a year, I've been pulling out handfuls of foam and filler, all of it disposed in the metal chamber pot where I piss and shit and, when the flu makes the rounds, get sick. I wrap my hand around a coil of cotton and pull; inch by inch, all those stolen linens are revealed, torn and braided, made strong to hold my weight. By now, the rope is nearly forty feet long.

I spend the rest of the evening making careful tears, using the edge of the dagger pin, now blunted nearly useless, to poke and tear holes in the fabric. No point in moving quickly.

There is nowhere to go, nothing else to do.

By the time I receive my daily dinner ration, I've finished working. I stuff the rope back in its hiding place, pushing, working it through the opening: a reverse birth. When I'm finished, I eat the food without tasting it, which is probably a blessing. Then I lie on my cot until the lights go off abruptly. The whimpering begins, the muttering and the occasional scream of someone gripped in a nightmare or, perhaps, waking from a pleasant dream only to discover he is still here. Strangely, I've learned to find the nighttime sounds almost comforting.

Eventually, my mind brings me memories of Lena, and then visions of the sea; at last, I sleep.

*then*

There was no resistance back then; there was no consciousness, yet, that we needed to resist. There were promises of peace and happiness, a relief from instability and confusion. A path and a place for all. A way to know, always, that your road was the right one. People were flocking to get cured the way they had once flocked to churches. The streets were papered with signs pointing the way to a better future. A central bank; jobs and marriages designed to fit like gloves.

And a life designed to slowly strangle.

But there was an underground: Brain Shops, someone who knew someone who could get you a fake ID for the right price; another person who could hook up an intercity bus ticket; someone else who rented basement space to anyone who wanted to disappear.

In Boston I stayed in the basement apartment of an older couple named Wallace. They weren't cured; they missed the age cutoff even when the procedure became mandatory, and were allowed to die in peace, in love. Or would have been allowed to – I heard several years later that they had been busted for harboring runaways, people who were dodging the cure, and spent the last few years of their lives in jail.

A path and a place for everyone, and for the people who disagree, a hole.

I should never have stolen his wallet. But that's the problem with love – it acts on you, works through you, resists your attempts to control. That's what made it so frightening to the lawmakers: love obeys no laws other than its own.

That's what has always made it frightening.

The basement was accessible only through a narrow alleyway that ran between the Wallaces' house and their neighbor's; the door was concealed behind a pile of junk that had to be carefully navigated each time we entered or left. Down a steep flight of stairs was a large, unfinished room: mattresses on the floor, a wild jumble of clothing, and a small toilet and sink, made semiprivate behind a folding screen. The ceiling was crisscrossed with metal pipes and plastic tubes and wiring, so it looked like someone's intestines tacked above us. It was ugly, freezing and smelled like dirty feet, and I loved it. In my short time there, I made two good friends: Misha, who hooked me up with Rawls and was trying to get me fake papers, too; and Steff, who taught me how to pick pockets and showed me all the best places to do it.

That is how I knew the name of the man I would someday marry: I stole his wallet. The slight touch, my hands across his chest, the momentary contact — it was long enough to feel for it in his jacket, slip it into my pocket and run.

I should have dumped the wallet and kept the cash, as Steff had taught me to do. But even then love was working on me, making me stupid and curious and careless. Instead I took the wallet back to the crash pad with me and spread out its contents carefully, greedily, on my mattress, like a jeweler bending over her diamonds. One government ID card, pristine, printed with the name conrad haloway. One credit card, gold, issued by the National Bank. One loyalty card at Boston Bean, stamped three times. A copy of his medical certification; he'd been cured exactly six months earlier. Forty-three dollars, which was a fortune to me.

And, tucked into one of the empty credit card flaps, distorting the leather slightly: one silver dagger pin, the size of a child's finger.

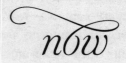

*now*

Three days after Thomas brings me the note telling me to wait, he comes again. This time he is carrying nothing. He merely slides open the door, enters my cell, cuffs me and hauls me to my feet.

'Let's go,' he says.

'Go where?' I ask.

'Don't ask questions.' He speaks loudly, no doubt so that the other prisoners will hear. He shoves me roughly toward the door, out into the narrow corridor that runs between the cells. Above us, the cameras set in the stone ceiling blink like small red eyes.

Thomas grabs my wrists and propels me forward. My shoulders burn. I have a momentary flash of fear: I'm so weak. How will I make it on my own, in the Wilds?

'What did I do?' I ask him.

'Breathe,' he answers. He puts on a good show. 'Didn't I tell you not to ask questions?' At one end of the corridor is the exit to the other wards; at the opposite end is the Tank. The Tank is only a cell, unused, but much smaller than the others, and fitted with nothing but a rusted metal ring hanging from the ceiling. If the residents of Ward Six are too loud, if they give trouble, they are strapped to the ring and whipped or hosed, or simply thrown in here to sit for days in darkness, soiling themselves when they need to go. But the hose is the worst: icy water, emerging with such force it takes your breath away, leaves you blackened and bruised.

Thomas does everything exactly as he should. He cuffs me to the ceiling, and for a moment, as he reaches above my head, we're so close that I can smell the coffee on his breath.

I feel a deep ache in my stomach, a sudden, wrenching pain; Thomas, for all the risks he is taking, still belongs to the other-world, of bus stops and convenience stores and dawn breaking over the horizon; of summer days and driving rains and wood fires in the winter.

For a moment, I hate him.

Once he locks the door, he turns to me.

'We don't have much time, so listen carefully,' he says. And just like that, my hatred evaporates, is replaced by a rush of feeling. Skinny Thomas, the boy I used to see sometimes hanging around the house, careful to pretend to be reading. How did he become this pudgy, hard-faced man, with hair gelled over a pink scalp, with lines etched deep into his face?

That's what time does: we stand stubbornly like rocks while it flows all around us, believing that we are immutable

– and all the time we're being carved, and shaped, and whittled away.

'It will happen soon. As early as this week. Are you ready?'

My mouth is dry. The rope is still too short by seven feet. But I nod. I can make the drop, and with a little luck, I'll hit a deep spot in the water.

'You'll go north from the river, then head east when you hit the old highway. There will be scouts looking for you. They'll take care of you. Got it?'

'North from the river,' I say. 'Then east.'

He nods. He looks almost sorry, and I can tell he thinks I won't make it. 'Good luck, Annabel.'

'Thank you,' I say. 'I can never repay you . . .'

He shakes his head. 'Don't thank me.' For a second we stand there, staring at each other. I try to see him as he once was: the boy Rachel loved. But I can hardly remember Rachel, now, as she was when I last saw her. Strangely, I can more easily picture her as a girl, always a little bossy, always demanding to know *why* she couldn't stay up and *what was the point* of eating green beans and *what if* she didn't want to get paired, anyway? And when Lena came along, she bossed her around, too; Lena trotted behind her like a puppy, eyes wide, observing, her fat thumb stuck in her mouth.

My girls. I know that I will never see them again. For their own safety, I can't.

But there is a small, stubborn, stone part of me that still hopes.

Thomas picks up the hose coiled in the corner. 'I told them you needed to be punished, so we could talk,' he says. He looks almost sick as he aims the nozzle at me.

My stomach rolls. The last time I was hosed was years

ago. I cracked a rib, and for weeks I ran a fever of more than a hundred, floating in and out of vivid dreams of fire, and faces screaming at me through the smoke. But I nod.

'I'll make it quick,' he says. His eyes say: *I'm sorry.*

Then he turns on the water.

*then*

**T**he girl behind the register was giving me the fish eye.

'You don't got no ID?' she said.

'I told you, I left it at home.' I was starting to get antsy. I was hungry – I was always hungry back then – and I didn't like the way the girl was looking at me, with her big bug eyes and the patchwork gauze on her neck, almost showing off the procedure, like she was some war hero and this was her injury to prove it.

'Haloway your pair or something?' She turned his credit card over in her hands, like she'd never seen one.

'Husband,' I snapped. She shifted her eyes to the place where my procedural scar should have been, but I had carefully combed my hair forward and jammed a wool hat down over my ears, so my entire neck was concealed. I shifted my weight, then realized I was fidgeting too much.

Scene: IGA Market on Dorchester, three days after the bust at Rawls's. Piled on the conveyor belt between us, the source of all the tension: a tin of instant hot cocoa, two packets of dried noodles, ChapStick, deodorant, a bag of chips. The air smelled stale and yeasty, and after the brutal winds of the streets, the store felt as hot as a desert, and as dry.

Why did I use his card? To this day, I don't know. I don't know whether I was getting overconfident or whether, just for a moment, I wanted to pretend: pretend that I wasn't a runaway, pretend that I wasn't squatting in an unfinished basement with six other girls, pretend that I had a home and a place and a pair, just like she did, just like everyone was supposed to.

Maybe I was already a little tired of freedom.

'We're not supposed to take cards without an ID,' she said after a long minute. I'll never forget her: those black bangs, the eyes as incurious, as flat, as marbles. 'If you want, I can call the manager.' She said it like she'd be doing me a favor.

Alarm bells went off in my head. Manager meant authority meant trouble. 'You know what? Forget it.'

But she had already swiveled around. 'Tony! Hey, Tony! Anybody know where Tony went?' Then she turned back to me, exasperated. 'Give me a second, okay?'

It was then: a split-second decision, the moment she left the register and went looking for Tony – a thirty, maybe forty-second reprieve. Without thinking, I stuffed the ChapStick in my pocket, pushed the chips and the noodles inside my jacket, and took off. I was a few feet from the door when I heard her yelling. So close to the street, to the blast of cold air and people bundled and indistinguishable. Three feet, then two . . .

A security guard materialized in front of me. He gripped me by the shoulders. He smelled like beer.

He said, 'Where do you think you're going, little lady?'

Within two days, I was on a bus back to Portland. This time my sister, Carol, was with me – and, for extra insurance, a member of the Juvenile Regulatory Commission, a skinny nineteen-year-old with a face full of pimples, hair like a tuft of sea grass and a wedding ring.

I knew Carol wouldn't be able to keep her mouth shut for long – she never had been able to – and as soon as we had pulled away from the bus terminal, she rounded on me.

'What you did was selfish,' she said. Carol was only sixteen at the time – we were born almost exactly a year apart – but even then she could have passed for forty. She carried a purse, an actual purse, and wore red leather gloves, square-toed black boots and jeans she actually ironed. Her face was narrower than mine, and her nose was upturned, as though it disapproved of the rest of her features and was trying to distinguish itself from them. 'Do you know how worried Mom and Dad are? And how embarrassed?'

My mother had been one of the first volunteers to be cured. She'd had the procedure even before it was federally mandated. After three decades in a marriage with my father – who was charming and loud when he was sober, mean and loud when he was drunk, and a philanderer whenever he could get his hands on a woman who would sleep with him – she had welcomed the cure like a beggar welcomes food, water and the promise of warmth. She'd bullied Dad into it too, and I had to admit, he was better for it. Calmer. Less angry. And he hardly drank anymore either. He hardly did anything anymore, since he'd been air-traffic control most his life – except sit in front of the TV or fiddle downstairs at his workbench, playing with old machine parts and radio equipment.

'Which is it?' I blew my breath onto the window, drew a star inside the condensation with my finger, then wiped it off.

Carol frowned. 'What?'

'Are they worried? Or are they embarrassed?' I blew again, and drew a heart this time.

'Both.' Carol reached out quickly and smudged the heart away. 'Stop that.' A look of fear flashed across her face.

'No one's looking,' I said. I leaned my head against the window, feeling suddenly exhausted. I was going home. No more bumping up against commuters, fumbling for easy picks, feeling the mix of shame and elation when a target worked out. No more peeing behind a folding screen in the middle of the night, trying not to wake anyone else up. I'd be cured right away, probably by the end of the week.

A small part of me was glad. There's always some relief in giving up.

'Why do you have to be so difficult?' Carol said.

I turned to look at her. My kid sister. We'd never been close. I'd wanted to love her, really. But she had always been too different, too cautious, likely to tell, impossible to play with.

'Don't worry,' I said. 'I won't give you any trouble again.'

I slept for most of the trip back to Portland, my hands tucked in my jacket and my forehead resting against the window, and the ID of Conrad Haloway cupped in my right palm.

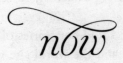

*now*

I've been on Ward Six for eleven years, with nothing but old stories, old words, for comfort. Scratching my way through minutes that feel like years, and years that have run by me like sand, like waste.

But now, waiting for Thomas to give me the signal, I find I have no patience left.

I remember that's how it was when I was pregnant with Lena. The last two weeks seemed longer than the rest of the months combined. I was so fat and my ankles were so swollen, it took energy just to stand. But I couldn't sleep, couldn't wait, and in the dark hours, after Rachel and my husband were asleep, I walked. I paced the room that would soon be hers back and forth: twelve steps across, twenty on the diagonal. I kneaded my feet on the carpet. I held my stomach, tight as a bowl, with both hands, and felt her gentle stirrings, her faint heartbeat pulsing under my fingertips like a distant drum.

And I spoke to her. I told her stories of who I'd been and who I'd wanted to be and the world she was about to enter and the world that had come before.

I said I was sorry.

I remember one time I turned and saw Conrad standing in the doorway. He stared at me, and in that moment the wordless thing passed between us, the thing that wasn't quite love but was so close I could believe in it sometimes – maybe a kind of understanding.

'Come to bed, Bells,' was all he said.

Now I find I must walk as well. I can't lie down anyway: the hose left bruises on my legs and spine, and even the touch of the sheet is painful. I can hardly bring myself to eat, but I know I must. Who knows how long I'll be out in the Wilds before the scouts find me, or if they even will? I have nothing but a pair of cotton slippers and a cotton jumpsuit. And the snow lies in heavy drifts along the frozen river; the trees will be bare, the animals in hiding.

If I can't find help, I'll die within two, three days. Better to die out there, though, in the world I have always loved – even now, after all it has done to me.

Three days pass with no word. Then a fourth and a fifth. The disappointment is constant, suffocating. When the sixth day passes with no sign from Thomas, I begin to lose hope. Maybe he has been found out. Another day goes by. I get angry. He must have forgotten about me.

My bruises have turned to starbursts, big explosions of

improbable colors, yellows and greens and purples. I'm no longer worried or angry. All my hope, the energy that I've been eking from thoughts of escape, abandons me at once. I lose even the desire to walk.

I'm filled with black thoughts: Thomas never intended to help me. The planned escape, the braiding of the rope, the scouts — all of it has been a dream, a fantasy that has kept me going all these years.

I stay in bed, don't bother to get up except when I have to relieve myself, and when at last the dinner tray is shoved in through a narrow slot in the door.

And then I freeze: underneath the small plastic bowl filled with pasta cooked into a lump is a small square of paper. Another note.

Thomas has written in all caps: *TONIGHT. BE READY.*

My stomach goes into my throat, and I'm worried I might be sick. Suddenly the thought of leaving these walls, this room, seems impossible. What do I know about the world outside? What do I know about the Wilds, and the resistance that survives there? When I was taken, I had only just begun my involvement with the movement. A meeting here, a document passed from hand to hand there . . .

I've been dreaming of escape for eleven years, and now, when the time has finally come, I know I'm not ready.

*then*

I didn't know, at first, that the cure hadn't worked.

Installed in my old bedroom at my parents' house, forbidden from seeing my friends, from leaving the house without permission and without Carol as an escort, I was as good as dead. Shuffling from the bed to the shower, watching the same news on TV, listening to the same music piping from the radio. This was what being cured was like: like being in a fishbowl, circling always inside the same glass.

I did what I was told, helped my parents with the chores, reapplied to college, since my admission had been rescinded once the facts of my time in Boston became public. I wrote letters of apology: to countless committees, to public officials, to my neighbors, to faceless bureaucrats with long, meaningless titles.

Slowly I earned back certain freedoms. I could go to the store by myself. I could go to the beach, too. I was able to see old friends, although most of them were forbidden from seeing me. And all that time, my heart was like a dull hammer in my chest.

It was a full six months before the Portland Evaluation Committee as it was called then, decided I was ready to be paired. The Marriage Stability Act had just been passed, and the system was still in its infancy. I remember that my mother and I had to go down to CORE, the Center for Organization, Research, and Education, to receive my results, and for the first time since I'd returned to Portland, I was filled with something like excitement. Except it was the bad kind, the kind that turns your stomach and makes your own spit taste a little like throw-up.

Dread.

I don't remember receiving the slender folder containing my results, but I know we were outside, in the car, before I could bring myself to open it. Carol was with us, in the backseat. 'Who'd you get?' she kept saying. But I couldn't read the names, couldn't make the words stand still on the page. The letters kept floating, drifting off the margins, and every picture looked like a collection of abstract shapes. For a minute, I thought I was losing my mind.

Until I reached my eighth recommended pair: Conrad Haloway. Then I *knew* I was losing my mind.

The picture was the same one he had used for his government ID – which I still kept, tucked at the bottom of my underwear drawer, concealed within a sock. Next to the picture were the basic facts of his life: where he was born, what school he'd attended, his various scores, his work history, details about his family and a psychological and social stability rank.

I felt a sudden surge, like my insides had been powered off, dusty and useless, for the past six months. Now they came online all at once: my heart beating up into my mouth, chest tight, lungs squeezing, squeezing.

'This one,' I said, trying to keep my voice steady. I pointed, placed a finger directly on his forehead between his eyes. The picture was black-and-white, but I remembered them perfectly: light brown, like hazelnut skins.

My mother leaned over me to look. 'He's a bit old, isn't he?'

'He's only just moved to Portland,' I said. 'He's been in service to the engineering corps. Working on the walls. See? It says so.'

My mother smiled tightly. 'Well, it's your choice, of course.' She reached over and patted me awkwardly on the knee. Even before her cure, she had never been affectionate; no one had ever touched in my family, unless it was my father taking a swing at my mom when he was drunk. 'I'm proud of you.'

Carol leaned forward into the front seat. 'He doesn't *look* like an engineer,' was all she said.

I turned my face to the window. On the drive home, I repeated his name to myself like a private rhythm: Conrad, Conrad, Conrad. My secret music. My husband. I felt something loosen inside my chest. His name warmed me. It spread through my mind, through my whole body, until I could feel the syllables in my fingertips, and all the way down to my toes. Conrad.

That's when I knew, without a doubt, that the cure hadn't worked at all.

*now*

The light goes out, and the nighttime noises begin on the ward: the murmurs and moans and screams.

I remember other noises – the sounds of outside: frogs singing, throaty and mournful; crickets humming an accompaniment. Lena as a young girl, her palms cupped carefully to contain a firefly, shrieking with laughter.

Will I recognize the world outside? Would I recognize Lena, if I saw her?

Thomas said he would give me the signal. But at least an hour passes with nothing – no sign, no further word. My mouth is dry as dust.

I am not ready. Not yet. Not tonight. My heartbeat is wild and erratic. I'm sweating already and shaking, too.

I can barely stand.

How will I run?

A jolt goes through me as the alarm system kicks on without warning: a shrill, continuous howl from downstairs, muffled through layers of stone and cement. Doors slam; voices cry out. Thomas must have tripped one of the alarms in a lower ward. The guards will go rushing for it, suspecting an attempted breakout or maybe a homicide.

That's my cue.

I stand up and shove the cot aside, so the hole in the wall is revealed: a tight squeeze, but big enough to fit me. My makeshift rope is coiled on the floor, ready to go, and I thread one end through the metal ring on the door, knot it as tightly as I can.

I'm not thinking anymore. I'm not afraid, either.

I toss the free end of the rope out through the hole, hear it snap once in the wind. For the first time since I was imprisoned, I thank God that the Crypts is windowless, at least on this side.

I go headfirst through the hole, wriggling when my shoulders meet resistance. Soft, wet stone rains down on my neck. My nose is full of the smell of spoiled things.

Good-bye, good-bye.

The alarm still wails, as though in response.

Then my shoulders are through and I'm upside down over a dizzying drop: forty-five feet at least, to the black and frozen river, motionless, reflecting the moon. And the rope, like a spun thread of white water, running vertically toward freedom.

I make a grab for the rope. I pull, hand over hand, sliding my body, my legs, through the jagged hole in the rock.

And then I fall.

My legs leave the lip of rock, and I swing a wild half circle, kicking into the air, crying out. I stop with a jerk, right side up, the rope coiled around my wrists. Stomach in my throat. The alarm is still going: high-pitched, hysterical.

Air, air, nothing but air. I'm frozen, unable to move up or down. I have a sudden memory of a spring cleaning the year before I was taken, and a giant spiderweb uncovered behind the standing mirror in the bedroom. Dozens of insects were bound, immobile, in white thread, and one had only just been caught – it was still struggling feebly to get out.

The alarm stops, and the ensuing silence is as loud as a slap. I have to move. I can hear the roar of the river now, and the shush of the wind through the leaves. Slowly I inch downward, wrapping my legs around the rope, swinging, nauseous. There's a pressure on my bladder, and my palms are burning. I'm too afraid to be cold.

Please let the rope hold.

Thirty feet from the river I lose my grip and free-fall several feet before catching myself. The force of my stop makes me cry out, and I bite down on my tongue. The rope lashes in the wind.

But I'm still safe. And the rope holds.

Inch by inch. It seems to take forever. Hand over hand. I don't even notice that my palms are bleeding until I see smears of red on the linens. But I feel no pain. I'm beyond pain now, numb from exhaustion. I'm weaker, even, than I'd feared.

Inch by inch.

And then, all at once, I'm at the end of the rope, and seven feet below me is the frozen Presumpscot, a blackened surface of rotted logs and rocks webbed with ice. I have no choice but to drop and pray for a good landing, try to avoid the water and make it into the drifts, white as a pillow, piled up on the banks.

I let go.

I kept up my end of the bargain. I gave my family no trouble. In the months leading up to the marriage ceremony, I said yes when I was supposed to and did what I was told.

But all the time, love grew inside me like a delicious secret.

It was exactly that way later, when I was pregnant first with Rachel, and then Lena. Even before the doctors confirmed it, I could always tell. There were the normal changes: the swollen, tender breasts; a sharpening sense of smell; a heaviness in my joints. But it was more than that. I could always *feel* it – an alien growth, the expansion of something beautiful and other and also entirely mine. A private constellation: a star growing inside my belly.

If Conrad remembered the skinny, frightened girl he'd

held for one brief moment on a frigid Boston street corner, he showed no signs of it when we met. From the beginning, he was polite, kind, respectful. He listened to me, and asked questions about what I thought, what I liked and what I didn't. He told me once, early on, that he liked engineering because he enjoyed the mechanics of making things work – structures, machines, anything. I know he often wished that people were more easily decoded.

That's, of course, what the cure was for: for flattening people into paper, into biomechanics and scores.

A year before Conrad died, he got the diagnosis: a tumor the size of a child's thumb was growing in his brain. It was sudden and totally unexpected. The doctors said bad luck.

I was sitting next to his hospital bed when he suddenly sat up, confused from a dream. Even as I tried to urge him back against the pillows, he looked at me with wild eyes.

'What happened to your leather jacket?' he asked.

'Shh,' I said, trying to soothe him. 'There's no leather jacket.'

'You were wearing it the first time I saw you,' he said, frowning slightly. Then he sagged suddenly back against the pillows, as though the effort of speaking had exhausted him. And I sat next to him while he slept, gripping his hand, watching the sun revolve in the sky outside the window and the patterns of light shifting on his sheet.

And I felt joy.

Conrad always held my head – lightly, with both hands – when we kissed. He wore glasses for reading, and when he was thinking hard about something, he would polish them. His hair was straight except for a bit that curled behind his left ear, just above his procedural scar. Some of this I observed right away; some of it I learned much later.

But from the beginning, I knew that in a world where destiny was dead, I was destined, forever, to love him. Even though he didn't – though he couldn't – ever love me back.

That's the easy thing about falling: there is only one choice after that.

*now*

I count three seconds of air. Then a blast of cold and a force like a fist, driving the breath from me, pummeling me forward. I hit bottom, and pain shoots up my ankle, and then the cold is everywhere, all at once, obliterating all other thoughts. For a minute, I can't breathe, can't get air, don't know which way is up or down. Just cold, everywhere and in all directions.

Then the river shoves me upward, spits me out, and I come up gasping, flailing, as ice breaks around me with a noise like a dozen rifles firing at once. Stars spin above me. I manage to make it to the edge of the river, and I slosh into the shallows, shivering so hard my brain feels like it's bouncing in my skull, coughing up water. I sit forward, cup my hand to the water and drink through frozen fingers. The water is sweet, slightly gritty with dirt, delicious.

I haven't felt the wind, truly felt it, in eleven years.

It's colder than I remember.

I know I have to move. North from the river. East from the old highway.

I take one last look at the looming silhouette of the Crypts. Free. I'm free. The word brings with it such a surge of joy, I have to consciously stop from crying out. I'm not safe yet.

Beyond the Crypts, I know, is the old, dusty road that leads to the bus stop – and beyond that, the gray sludge of the service road, which extends all the way on-peninsula and eventually merges with Congress Street. And then: Portland, my Portland, gripped on three sides by water, nestled like a jewel on a small spit of land.

Somewhere, Lena is sleeping. Rachel, too. My own jewels, the stars I carry with me. I know that Rachel was cured, and out of reach to me now. Thomas told me so.

But Lena . . .

My littlest . . .

*I love you. Remember.*

*And someday, I will find you again.*

# RAVEN

**H**ere are the top three things I've learned in my twenty-two years on the planet:

1. Never wipe your butt with poison ivy.
2. People are like ants: just a few of them give all the orders. And most of them spend their lives getting squashed.
3. There are no happy endings, only breaks in the regular action.

Of all of them, number three is really the only one you have to keep in mind.

'This is stupid,' Tack says. 'We shouldn't be doing this.'

I don't bother replying. He's right, anyway. This *is* stupid, and we *shouldn't* be doing it. But we are.

'If anything goes wrong, we abort,' Tack says. 'I mean anything. I won't miss out on Christmas for this shit.'

'Christmas' is code for the next big mission. We've only heard rumors about it so far. We don't know when, and we don't know where. All we know is that it's coming.

I feel a sudden wave of nausea, a tide rolling up to my throat, and swallow it.

'Nothing will go wrong,' I say, even though of course I can't know that. That's what I said about migration this year. *Nobody dies,* I said, over and over, like a prayer.

I guess God wasn't listening.

'Border patrol,' I say, as though Tack can't see the solid cement wall, darkened by rain, and the checkpoints ahead. He eases on the brakes. The van is like an old man: always hacking and shuddering and taking forever to do what you want it to. But as long as it gets us where it needs to go.

'We could have been halfway to Canada by now,' Tack says, which is, of course, an exaggeration. That's how I know he's upset. Tack hardly ever exaggerates. He says exactly what he means, only when he means it.

It's one of the reasons I love him.

We get through the border without any trouble. Eight years of living in the Wilds and four of working actively with the resistance, and I've learned that half the country's security is for show. It's all a big song and dance, a stage production: a way of keeping the tiny ants in line, cowed by fear, heads bent to the dirt. Half the guards are barely trained. Half the walls unpatrolled. But it's the image that matters, the impression of constant surveillance, of containment.

Ants are driven by fear.

Tack is quiet as we drive down the West Side Highway, empty of traffic. The river and the sky are the same slate-gray color, and the rain sends sheets of water across the road. The clouds have the same low-down, swollen-belly look they did on the day, years ago, when I Crossed.

The day I found her.

I still can't say her name.

I used to be an ant too. Back when I lived before, back when I had a different name, back when the only scar I had was a small, thin fissure on my abdomen, where the doctors had had to remove my appendix.

I can still remember my old house: the gauzy curtains that smelled like gardenias and plastic; the carpet sprinkled with baking soda and vacuumed daily; the quiet, heavy as a hand. My father liked quiet. Noise made the buzzing start up in his brain – like a storm of bees, he once told me. The louder the buzzing got, the more he couldn't think. The more he couldn't think, the angrier he got. Until he had to break, he had to stop it, he had to smash back all that sound with a fist, until there was quiet again.

We were a whirlpool, circling constantly around him, trying to keep the buzzing from coming back.

I almost drowned in that house.

'Raven?'

I turn to Tack, realizing he's been trying to get my attention. 'What?' I say, a little too sharply.

'Here?'

Tack has slowed down in front of a parking lot on Twenty-

Fourth Street, unattended, empty except for two cars. The street is lined with identical apartments, stiff as sentinels, blinds pulled down against the rain: a whole street of darkened red brick and bird-shit-stained front steps and blindness.

'We're early,' he says.

'She had seven hours on us, at least,' I say.

'Still, if she was walking . . .' He shrugs.

'So we wait,' I say. 'Turn left on Nineteenth. I want to scout the block.'

Northeastern Medical, the clinic where Julian Fineman is scheduled to die, is on Eighteenth Street; we can thank the radio for letting that little detail slip. I'm surprised there's not more press. Then again, they might be inside already, angling for a good view. Tack circles the block twice – not enough times to look suspicious, in case anyone is watching – and we talk over the plan together. He helps me think it out, then parks and waits for me while I walk the perimeter on foot, scanning the entrances and the exits, checking out nearby buildings, potential pitfalls, dead ends and hiding places.

Several times I have to stop, breathe, struggle not to puke.

'Did you find a place for the backpack?' Tack asks when I climb back into the van.

I nod. He inches carefully into nonexistent traffic. Another thing I love about Tack: how careful he is. Meticulous, in some ways. And in others, totally free – quick to laugh, full of crazy ideas. Hardly anyone gets to see that side of him. How he speaks in a rush when he's excited. How he likes to say the word *love*, over and over.

*Love. I love you. I'll always love you, my love. You are the love of my life.*

We keep these things for each other, the deepest parts. In

valid cities it's those places that get stomped out first, even before the cure – the wounds and weirdness and the pieces we carry like misshapen gifts, waiting for a person to welcome them.

*Love* is still hard for me to say sometimes, even when we're alone, even after all this time. So we've made up our own language, in the way we press chest to chest and the way we touch noses when we kiss. I get to say his name – his real name. A name that brings a taste of sunshine, and of sunshine raising mist from the trees, and of mist reaching toward the sky.

His secret name, which belongs to me, and to him, and to no one else.

*Michael*.

Did I ever tell her I loved her?

I don't know.

I can't remember.

I thought it every day.

*I'm sorry.*

The nausea is near constant now. It rolls me up and down. Thinking of her is too much, and the acid comes up from my stomach and burns the back of my throat.

'Pull over,' I tell Tack.

I puke behind a car that looks like it hasn't been moved in years, next to a small pharmacy, its battered blue awning pooling the rain. The vertical neon sign advertising consultation and diagnosis is dark, but a small orange sign hangs beyond the grungy door: open. For a second I debate going in, making up some story, trying to get another test, just to be sure. But it's too risky, and I need to stay focused on Lena.

I tent my jacket above my head as I run back to the van, feeling a little better now that I've thrown up.

The gutters are running with trash, whipping small bits of paper and disposable cups into the drain. I hate the city. Wish I was out with the rest of the group at the warehouse, packing up, counting heads, measuring supplies. Wish I was anywhere, really – fighting through the Wilds, which are always changing, always growing; fighting the Scavengers, even.

Anywhere but this towering gray city, where even the sky is held at bay.

Where we are as small as ants.

The van smells like mildew and tobacco and, weirdly, like peanut butter. I crack open a window.

'What was that about?' Tack asks.

'Didn't feel good,' I say, staring straight ahead, willing him not to ask any more questions. Two straight weeks of getting sick in the mornings. At first I thought it was just the stress – Lena captured, the whole plan out of our hands. Waiting. Watching. Hoping she'd get it right.

Patience was never my strong suit.

'You don't look good,' he says. And then, 'What's going on, Raven? Are you—?'

'I'm fine,' I say quickly. 'My stomach's just fucked up, that's all. It's that goddamn jerky we've been eating.'

Tack relaxes a little. He stops white-knuckling the wheel, and the muscle in his jaw goes still. I feel a wave of guilt, a surge even worse than the nausea. Lying is a defense, like a porcupine's quills or a bear's claws. And my time in the Wilds has made me very good at it. But I don't like lying to Tack.

He's practically the only person I have left.

\*        \*        \*

'Is she yours?'

Those were Tack's first words to me. I can still see him the way he was then: skinnier, even, than he is now. Big hands. Two nose rings. Eyes half-closed but alert, like a lizard's; hair falling practically to the bridge of his nose. Sitting in the corner of the sickroom, hands and ankles bound. Pockmarked with mosquito bites and bloody with scratches.

I'd been in the Wilds for only a month. I was lucky, and found my way to a homestead within six hours of crossing from Yarmouth. Double lucky, actually. Only a week later, the homestead relocated, moved into New Hampshire, just south of Rochester. Rumors of a raid on the Wilds had everyone jumpy. I'd made it just in time.

I had to. Blue was barely alive, and I had no way of feeding her. I'd run in a panic, blind to anything but the need to disappear; had no supplies, no knowledge, no hope of making it on my own. My shoes were too tight and left raw, bloody blisters the size of quarters after only a few hours of walking. I didn't know how to navigate. Didn't keep track of where I was going. Got thirsty but didn't think of sipping from a stream because I was worried it would make me sick.

Idiot. If I hadn't wandered into the homestead, I would have died. And she would have too.

Little baby Blue.

I hadn't believed in God since I was a little kid and saw my dad take my mom by the hair and slam her face-first into the kitchen counter, watched a spray of blood on the linoleum and saw one of her teeth skitter across the floor, white and shiny as a die. I knew then there was no one watching over us.

But my first night in the Wilds, when the forest opened

up like a jaw and I saw lights glowing fuzzily in the darkness, small halos beyond the rain, and heard voices – when Grandma put a blanket around my shoulders, and Mari, twenty-two years old, who'd just given birth to her second stillborn, took Blue in her arms and to her breast and cried silently the whole time she was suckling, when I knew we'd both been saved – that night, I thought I knew God, just for a second.

'I'm not supposed to talk to you,' I said to Tack. Only I didn't know his name then. He didn't have a name then. Didn't have a group, or a homestead; didn't belong anywhere. We called him the Thief.

The Thief laughed. 'You aren't, huh? What about all the freedom on the other side of the walls?'

'You're a Scavenger,' I said, even though I hardly knew what the term meant. I hadn't seen one yet, thank God, and wouldn't for two years, during a relocation that wiped out half our number. 'I don't want to talk to you.'

He flinched. 'I'm not a Scavenger.' Then he lifted his chin and stared at me. That was the first time I realized he was probably my age. His clothes, the dirtiness of him, his attitude – I'd assumed he was older. 'I'm not anything.'

'You're a thief,' I said, looking away. Only a month in the Wilds – I hadn't even begun to shake my fear of them. Boys.

He shrugged. 'I'm a survivor.'

'You were stealing our food,' I said. I didn't add: *Everyone thought I was to blame*. 'That makes you a Scavenger in my opinion.'

For the past several weeks, the homesteaders had noticed supplies gone missing, some traps empty that should have been full, a jug or two of clean water mysteriously emptied overnight. The group had grown tense, suspicious, and I became the prime suspect. I was the newest, after all. No one knew who I was or where I'd come from or what I was about, and the thefts had started soon after I'd arrived with Blue.

So this guy named Gray, who was kind of the group leader at the time, had started surveillance without telling anyone. In the middle of the night he got out of bed and circulated to all the snares and traps, checked the storerooms, made sure everyone from the homestead was exactly where they should be. On the second day of his rounds, he caught Tack wrestling a rabbit out of one of our traps. Stealing. Tack nearly put a knife through Gray, trying to escape. But he missed and just sliced off a chunk of Gray's shoulder blade, and Gray managed to shout and pin Tack to the ground, and since then he'd been our prisoner and everyone had been debating what to do about him.

'Welcome to freedom,' he said. And he spit. Right next to his feet, on the ground. 'Everyone has an opinion.'

I turned my attention back to Blue. Grandma had told me not to get too attached. *So many of them don't make it out here,* she'd said. But I was already attached. From the second I found her; from the second I felt the skating pressure of her heartbeat beneath her tiny ribs. I knew she was mine – my job, my duty to protect.

At first she'd barely taken any food from Mari, but after two weeks she was eating better and beginning to gain weight. When Mari nursed, I sat next to her, sometimes with an arm around Blue, like I could absorb them both. Like I was the one sending life out through my fingertips and into Blue's veins and heart and mouth. I kept Blue with me all the time.

Grandma gave me an old baby carrier, faded to a dull and genderless gray from so many washings, so I could strap her to my chest when I was helping the others with the rounds.

But then she'd gotten sick again. She fussed and wouldn't stay asleep for more than fifteen minutes at a time. Her nose was always running, and on the second day, her fever was so bad, I could feel the heat of her body when I held my hand six inches from her chest. She stopped feeding, and she cried for hours at a time. Everyone told me it was just a cold, and she'd get over it.

For three days, I'd been moving through a thick fog of exhaustion, a relentless tiredness like nothing I'd ever known. At night, I stayed awake and whispered to her, rocking her even as she tried to push me off, keeping her cool with wet cloths. We had moved, both of us, into the sickroom. Tack had been placed there too, temporarily, while the other home-steaders convened in the main room and talked about whether to let him go and trust that he wouldn't steal from us again, or whether he should be punished, even killed.

The law of the Wilds was just as harsh, in its way, as the law on the other side of the fence.

Tack watched me as I bent over Blue, murmuring to her, wiping the sweat from her forehead. She wasn't crying anymore. Her eyes were half-closed, and she barely stirred when I touched her. Her breathing was short and shallow.

'It's RSV,' Tack spoke up suddenly. 'She needs medicine.'

'You some kind of doctor?' I fired back. But I was scared. I wished she would cry, open her mouth, respond to me in any way. But she was just lying there, fighting for breath. And I knew then that it wasn't just a cold. Whatever she had was getting worse.

'My mother was a nurse,' Tack said calmly. This startled me. It was weird to think of the Thief, the wild and lawless boy, as having a mother – as having a past at all. I looked at him.

'Untie me,' he said, his voice low, convincing, 'and I'll help you.'

'Bullshit,' I said.

There's a part of me – a big part – that's hoping Lena won't show up. She might have gotten stuck at the border, or caught by a patrol without an ID. She might have gotten lost. She might just be too late. Then Tack and I won't have to get involved, won't risk a big fat stinking mess.

But we've trained her too well, and at a couple of minutes before 10 a.m., I spot her moving up the street, head down against the rain, which has petered out to a slow drizzle. She's wearing clothes that don't belong to her, except for the wind breaker, which she must have taken from the safe house. Still, her walk is unmistakable: light on her feet, kind of bouncing on her toes, as if she might break into a run at any second.

Tack spots her the same time I do and sinks down a little in the front seat, as if worried she might spot us. But she's totally focused. She barely pauses at the entrance to the clinic. She slips inside.

Any moment now. The air inside the van is humid, and my skin feels sticky. The windows are fogged from our breath. I feel another roll of nausea and fight it back. No time for that.

After a few minutes, Tack sighs and reaches for the jacket balled up on the seat between us. He shakes it out and shoves his arms, hard, into the sleeves. He looks funny in a suit jacket, like a bear dressed up in a costume for the circus. I would never tell him that, though.

'Ready?' he says.

'Don't forget this.' I pass him a small laminated ID. It's so old and stained, the picture is nearly indistinguishable – which is good, because its original owner, Dr Howard Rivers, was about twenty pounds heavier than Tack and had a decade on him.

Then again, Howard Rivers wasn't actually Howard Rivers, but Edward Kauffman, a respected doctor in Maine who worked to keep the *deliria* out of our schools and homes, who had ties to the governor, who subsidized medical centers in poorer parts of town. Secretly, though, he was a radical and controversial resister, famous for performing under-the-table abortions on uncureds who'd gotten pregnant and were desperate to conceal it.

Over the years he established identities for a dozen fake doctors so he could increase his shipments of medicine and antibiotics, which he then distributed to Invalids in the Wilds.

Edward Kauffman, the original, is dead now – has been dead for two years. He was outed in a police sting operation and executed only two weeks later. But many of his pseudonyms, his fake identities, survived. They're healthy and practicing still.

Tack clips the ID to his jacket. 'How do I look?' he says.

'Medical,' I answer.

He checks his reflection in the rearview and tries unsuccessfully to mash down his hair. 'Don't forget,' he says. 'Parking lot on Twenty-Fourth. I'll be waiting for you.'

'We'll be there,' I say, ignoring the weird feeling in my stomach. More than nausea. Nerves. I hate being nervous. It's a weakness. It reminds me of the person I used to be, and the ticking quiet of the old house, my father brewing, growing his anger like a storm.

Every time I have to kill someone, I pretend he has my father's face.

'Be careful, Rae.' For a second, I get a glimpse of Michael, the boy no one sees. Face open like a kid's. Scared. 'I wish you'd let me do the heavy lifting.'

'Where's the fun in that?' I press my fingers against my lips, bring them to his chest. It's our sign. Neither one of us is super touchy-feely, and besides, it's too risky to kiss in Zombieland. 'See you on the other side.'

'On the other side,' he parrots, then slips out of the van, jogging across the street pooled with rain.

I count off sixty seconds, make some last-minute adjustments to my gear, flip down the mirror and check my teeth. Feel for the gun concealed in my jacket and check the supplies in my right jeans pocket. All good. All there. Count another sixty seconds, which helps me ignore the nerves. Nothing to be afraid of.

I know what I'm doing. We all do. Too well.

Sometimes I imagine that Tack and I will just crap out – flake on the whole war, the struggle, the resistance. Say good-bye and see you never. We'll go up north and build a homestead together, far away from everyone and everything. We know how to survive. We could do it. Trap and hunt and fish for our food, grow what we can, pop out a whole brood of kids and pretend the rest of the world doesn't exist. Let it blow itself to pieces if it wants to.

Dreams.

It has been two and a half minutes. I open the van door

and hop down to the curb. The rain is nothing more than a mist now, but the gutters are still overflowing, swirling eddies of crushed coffee cups and cigarette butts and flyers.

When I push open the door to the clinic, it's like a different world: thick green carpet, and furniture polished so it shines. Big, showy clock in the corner, ticking away the minutes. Not a bad place to die, if you had to choose.

Tack is standing at reception, drumming his fingers against the desk. He barely glances at me when I come in.

'I'm so sorry, doctor.' The lab tech behind the desk is punching buttons frantically. Her fingers are fat and weighted down with rings that cut deep into her flesh. 'An inspection – today – there *must* be a mistake.'

'It's on the books,' Tack says, in a voice that belongs to someone older and fatter and cured. 'Every clinic is subjected to an annual regulatory—'

'Excuse me,' I say loudly, interrupting him, as I come toward the desk. I make sure to walk a little funny, just for show. Tack and I can laugh about it later. 'Excuse me,' I repeat, a little louder. Too loud for the space.

'You'll have to hold on,' the receptionist says to me, picking up the phone and angling her chin away from the receiver. She turns immediately back to Tack. 'I'm so sorry. You have no idea how embarrassed—'

'Don't be sorry,' he says. 'Just get somebody down here who can help me.'

'Hey.' I lean forward over the counter. 'Look, I'm talking to you.'

'Ma'am.' She's losing it. She's probably shitting bricks, thinking she's going to get the whole clinic shut down because she screwed up the review dates. 'I'm in the middle of something. If you have an appointment, you're going to have to sign in and take a seat in the—'

'I don't have an appointment.' I'm really putting it on, now, practically yelling. Tack does a good job of looking disgusted. 'And I won't wait. I got this rash, okay? It's driving me crazy. I can't hardly even sit.'

I undo my belt and start to hitch my pants down over my waist, like I'm about to moon her. Tack draws back with a noise of disgust, and the nurse slams down the phone and practically hurls herself around the desk.

'This way, ma'am, *please*.' She clamps a hand on my arm. I can smell the sweat underneath her perfume. She pilots me quickly out of the reception area – away from Dr Howard Rivers, medical inspector, where I can't do any harm, where I won't embarrass the clinic any further – and through a set of double doors into a long white hallway. I feel a hitch of excitement in my chest, a slight break, like I always do when a plan is going off like we expected. With my free hand I fumble in my right jeans pocket for the small glass bottle, uncork it with a thumb, let the contents spill out into the rag stuffed in my pocket. Acetone, bleach and heat.

Not as good as manufactured chloroform, but good enough.

'The doctor will be in to see you shortly,' she says, huffing from the exertion of piloting me forward. She practically shoves me into a small examination room and stands, breasts heaving against her uniform, with one hand on the doorknob. The hall behind her is empty. 'If you'll just wait here . . .'

'I hate waiting,' I say, and step forward, bringing the rag to her face.

She is very heavy as she goes down.

\*     \*     \*

*Untie me, and I'll help you.*

The words were stuck in my mind, a taunt and a promise. I didn't think I could trust him. And it would be a betrayal – of Grandma, and of the other homesteaders who had taken in Blue and me. If I got caught, if the Thief screwed us over, I'd have to pay for it. Maybe I'd get tied up in the sickroom, waiting for the group to decide what should be done with me.

But Blue wasn't getting any better.

I was so afraid – afraid of everything back then, just a skinny little shit who'd made a snap-dash decision to run away and who had no idea what she was doing. My dad had always told me I was stupid in the head, pathetic, one of the losers. And back then, maybe he was right.

I knew the Thief wasn't afraid. I could just tell. Wasn't afraid of me or the other homesteaders, wasn't afraid of dying.

When Blue started gurgling and rasping in her sleep – then went ten seconds at a time, still, not breathing, before taking in a gasp of air – I stole a knife from the kitchen and brought it back to the sickroom. My hands were shaking. I remember, because I kept thinking of my mom's hands, rattling her silverware, fluttering like birds, a wild, frantic part of her. I wondered if she'd been thinking of me at all since I'd left.

It was late. Everyone else was asleep – now that the Thief had been caught, even Gray didn't feel the need to patrol.

The Thief's smile was like a sickle blade in the dark. I squatted down in front of him.

'You promised,' I told him. 'You promised to help me.'

'Cross my heart and hope to die,' he said. I didn't like the sound of his voice – like he was laughing at me – but I cut him loose anyway, feeling sick the whole time, knowing Blue would die otherwise. Might die just the same.

He stood up, groaning a little. I hadn't realized how tall he was. I hadn't seen him except sitting or lying down since he was brought in. I took a step backward, flinching, when he raised his arms above his head.

His smile vanished, turned into something harder. 'You don't trust me, do you?' he said.

I shook my head. He extended his hand for the knife, and after a second's hesitation, I gave it to him.

'I'll be back by noon,' he said. My heart was beating hard in my throat, a rhythm saying, *Please, please. I'm counting on you.* He jerked his chin in Blue's direction. 'Keep her alive until then.'

Then he was gone, moving soundlessly through the darkened halls, vanishing into the shadows. And I sat holding Blue, with terror sitting like a black mist in my chest, and waited.

Lies are just stories, and stories are all that matter. We all tell stories. Some are more truthful than others, maybe, but in the end the only thing that counts is what you can make people believe.

I learned to tell stories from my mom. 'Your dad's not feeling well today,' she'd say. She'd say, *I had an accident.* She'd say, *Remember what happened. You're a clumsy girl. You walked into a door. You tripped and stumbled down a staircase.* My favorite story: *He doesn't mean to.*

She was so good at telling stories that I started to believe them after a while. Maybe I was clumsy. Maybe it was my fault, for provoking him.

Maybe he really didn't mean to.

There were stories, too, about a girl who got pregnant before her cure. Caroline Gormely – she lived down the street from me, in our neighborhood of boxy, identical-looking houses. Her parents only found out after she swallowed half a bottle of bleach and was taken to the emergency room. One day she was around, riding the bus home from school, pressing her nose to the glass, the window fogging with her breath. And one day she wasn't anymore.

My mom told me she'd been taken somewhere to be cured, shipped off to a different city where she could start again. Her parents had disowned her. She would likely end up working sanitation somewhere, never paired, carrying the blight of the disease around her like a scar. *You see what happens,* my dad said, *when you don't listen?*

*What about the baby?* I'd asked my mom.

She hesitated for only a second. *The baby will be taken care of,* she said. And she meant it: just not in the way I thought.

The lab tech's uniform is big on me, so big I feel like a kid playing dress-up. But it will work. I don't rush. A good story needs pacing, deliberateness. I take my time finding a small fabric mask, which I slip over my face, and rubber gloves. I lock the doorknob before I slip back out into the hall. No sense in risking the discovery of the nurse, who is now curled up on the linoleum, breathing deeply, like a child.

I clip her ID on my uniform, knowing no one will check it. You need to give people the broad strokes, the things they're expecting: the main characters and the buildup.

And the climax, of course. A good story always needs a climax.

None of the homesteaders blamed me for the Thief's escape, as I had worried they would, even after the kitchen knife was discovered to be missing. Everyone assumed he had broken out somehow, that he had managed to loosen the restraints himself and had stolen the knife before sneaking out. The hard-liners, the ones who had wanted to see him killed, gloated: he was no good, he might be back to murder them in their sleep, they'd have to keep constant tabs on the food stores now. Should have offed the no-good Scavenger when they'd had a chance.

I almost spoke up. I would have confessed, but I was too scared that I would get turned out, abandoned in the Wilds.

The Thief had promised to be back by noon, but noon came and went, and by the time the homesteaders were finished with their rounds and Blue's breathing sounded like a rattle in her chest, when she was breathing at all, I knew that he had lied to me. He would never be back, and Blue would die, and it was all my fault. I couldn't cry about it because I'd learned never to cry, even as a little girl. Crying was one of the things that set my dad off, just like laughing too loud, or smiling at a joke that didn't include him, or acting happy when he was miserable, or miserable when he was happy.

I remember Lu watched Blue while I went for some air, even though I could tell she didn't think it would do any good. Everyone was walking around me like I had some kind of disease, or like I was in detonator mode and might fracture at any second into shrapnel. That was the worst: knowing they thought she was going to die too.

I still wasn't used to the Wilds, and I didn't like them then. I was used to rules and fences, rivers of pavement and parking lots, order everywhere. The Wilds were vast and dark and unpredictable, and reminded me of back home and my dad's rage, hanging like a low weight over everything, leaving no room to breathe, pressing us into submission. Later, I learned that the Wilds did obey certain rules, did contain a certain kind of order – raw and bare and beautiful.

Only humans are unpredictable.

I remember: a high moon, the weight of fear, the strangle-squeeze of guilt. A cold wind, bringing unfamiliar smells.

The crack of a branch. A footstep.

And suddenly there he was: the Thief emerged from the woods, looking ten years older than he had when he left, soaking wet. He was carrying a backpack. For a second, I couldn't believe he was real. I thought I must be dreaming.

'Albuterol,' he said, lifting the backpack. 'For the girl. And supplies for the others. Penance for my crime.'

Tylenol, Sudafed, Band-Aids, antibiotics, bacitracin, Neosporin, penicillin. It was a jackpot. No one could believe that he'd returned. No one could believe that he'd risked his life, made a crossing to the other side, to stock up on supplies so desperately needed. He said nothing about the agreement we'd made. His earlier crimes were forgiven.

He told the homesteaders about a small, plain storage facility, minimally secure and totally unmarked, on the banks of the Cocheco River. The man who owned it, Edward Kauffman, was a sympathizer, and doled out medication and even certain treatments to uncureds on the sly. Tack had moved upstream, fighting a heavy current, and crossed just east of Kauffman's clinic. He'd had to hide out for a while before crossing back, however, waiting for a patrol to move on.

'How'd you know about the clinic?' I asked him.

'My sister,' he told me shortly. He didn't say, but I guessed:

she'd had some kind of procedure there, something he didn't want me to know about. Later on, I understood.

'Sharp as a tack, that one,' Grandpa announced after the Thief had finished speaking; and so the Thief received a name, and became one of us.

Beyond the waiting room, the hospital looks like any other: bleak, ugly, overly scrubbed. I don't like places that are too clean. It always makes me think about what's getting covered up and scrubbed off.

I walk, head down, not too quick, not too slow. Hardly anyone in the halls, and the only doctor I pass barely glances at me. Good. People mind their own business here.

I get a break when I hit the bank of elevators: a guy standing, tapping his foot, checking his watch, a poster boy for impatience, with a large camera slung around his neck and the look of someone who hasn't slept in a week. Press.

'You here for Julian Fineman?' is all I have to say.

'It's six, right? The woman at the front desk told me it was on six.' He must be in his thirties, but he has a big pimple right on the tip of his nose, angry as a blister. His whole vibe is a little like a pimple, actually: ready to explode.

I follow him into the elevator, reach out and punch six with a knuckle. 'It's six,' I say.

The first time I ever killed someone I was sixteen. It was almost two years since I'd escaped to the Wilds, and by then the homestead had changed. Certain people had left or died; others had showed up. We'd had a bad winter my first year, four weeks of almost straight snow, no hunting, no trapping, making do on scraps left over from the summer – dried strips of meat, and, when that ran out, plain rice. But worse than that was the freeze, the days snow piled up so quick and so heavy it wasn't safe to go outside; when the homestead reeked of unwashed bodies and worse; when the boredom was so bad it crawled down into your skin and made a constant itch.

Mari didn't make it past that winter. The second stillborn had hit her hard; even before the winter she sometimes spent days curled up on her cot, one arm crooked around the negative space where a baby should have been. That winter, it was like something brittle finally snapped inside of her, and one morning we woke up and found her swinging from a wooden beam in the food room.

It was snowing too hard to bring her up, so for two days we had to live alongside her body.

We lost Tiny, too, who went out one day to try and hunt, even though we told him it was no use and the animals wouldn't be out and it was too risky. But he was going crazy from being penned in so long, crazy from the constant hunger gnawing like a rat from the inside out. He never came back. Probably got lost and froze to death.

So my second year we decided to move. It was Gray's decision, actually, but we were all on board. Bram, who'd arrived earlier in the summer, told us about some homesteads farther south, friendly places where we would find shelter. In August, Gray sent out scouts to chart routes and look for campsites. In September, we started relocation.

The Scavengers hit in Connecticut. I'd heard stories about them, but never concrete stuff: more whispers and myths, like the monster stories my mom had told me as a kid to make me behave. *Shhh. Be quiet or you'll wake the dragon.*

It was late and I was sleeping when Squirrel, who was

scouting, gave the alarm: two shots fired into the darkness. But it was too late. Suddenly everyone was screaming. Blue – already big, beautiful, with the eyes of a grown-up and a pointed chin like mine – woke up bawling, terrified. She wouldn't leave the tent. She was clinging to the sleeping bag, kicking me off, saying, *No, no, no* over and over again.

By the time I managed to get her up, get her into my arms and out of the tents, I thought the world was ending. I'd grabbed a knife, but I didn't know what to do with it. I'd once skinned an animal and it had nearly made me puke.

I found out later that there were only four of them, but at the time it seemed like they were everywhere. That's one of their tricks. Chaos. Confusion. There was fire – two tents went up just like that, like two match heads exploding – and there were shots and people screaming.

All I could think was *run*. I had to run. I had to get Blue away from there. But I couldn't move. I felt terror like a cold weight inside me, rooting me in place, the same way it always had when I was a little girl – when my dad would come down the stairs, *stomp, stomp, stomp*, his anger like a blanket meant to suffocate us all. Watching from the corner while he kicked my mom in the ribs, in the face, unable to cry, unable to scream, even. For years I'd fantasized that the next time he touched me, or her, I'd stick a knife straight in through the ribs, all the way up to the handle. I'd thought about the blood bubbling from the wound and how good it would feel to know that he, like me, was made out of real stuff, bones and tissue, skin that could bruise.

But every time I was frozen, empty as a shell. Every time I did nothing but take it: red starburst explosions to the face, behind the eyes; pinches and slaps; hard shoves to the chest.

'Let's go, let's go!' Tack was shouting from the other side of the camp. I started running to him without thinking, without watching where I was going, still clotted up with panic, with Blue soaking my neck with snot and tears and my heart drilling out of my chest, and when the Scavenger came from the left I didn't even see him until he was swinging a club at my head.

I dropped Blue. Just let her fall to the ground. And I went down behind her, knees hard in the dirt, trying to shield her. I got a hand around her pajama bottoms and managed to pick her up and get her on her feet.

'Run,' I said. 'Go on.' I pushed her. She was crying, and I pushed her. But she ran, as well as she could, on legs that were still too short for her body.

The Scavenger drove a foot between my ribs, exactly the spot where my dad had fractured them when I was twelve. The pain made everything go black for a second, and when I rolled over on my back, everything was different. The stars weren't stars but a ceiling spotted with water stains. The dirt wasn't dirt but a nubby carpet.

And the Scavenger wasn't a Scavenger but Him. My dad.

Eyes small as cuts, fists as fat as leather belts, breath hot and wet in my face. His jaw, his smell, his sweat. He'd found me. He raised a fist and I knew it was starting all over again, that it would never stop, that he would never leave me alone and I would never escape.

That Blue would never be safe.

Everything went dark and silent.

I didn't know I'd reached for the knife until it was deep between his ribs.

*   *   *

That's all I've ever heard: silence. The times I've killed. The times I've had to kill. If there is a God, I guess he has nothing to say about it.

If there is a God, he must have gotten tired of watching a long time ago.

There is silence in Julian Fineman's execution room, except for the occasional *click-click* of a camera, except for the drone of the priest's voice. *But when Abraham saw that Isaac had become unclean, he asked in his heart for guidance . . .*

Silence like whiteness: like things painted over and concealed, or left unsaid.

Silence except for the *squeak, squeak* of my sneakers on the linoleum floor. The doctor turns to look at me, annoyed. Confused.

The first gunshot is very loud.

I'm remembering: all those years ago, sitting with Tack when he was newly named. The red-ember glow of the fire in the old woodstove, and Blue, breathing easier already, heavy in my arms. Sleep sounds from the other rooms, and somewhere above us, the hiss of the wind through the trees.

'You came back,' I said. 'I didn't think you would.'

'I wasn't going to,' he admitted. He looked different, wearing clothes Grandpa had found for him in the storeroom – much younger, much skinnier. His eyes were huge dark hollows in his face. I thought he was beautiful.

I hugged Blue a little closer. She was still hot, still fussing in her sleep. But her breaths came even and slow, and there was no trapped rattle in her chest. For the first time, it struck me that I'd been lonely. Not just at the homestead, where everyone was too busy surviving to worry about making friends, where most of the Invalids were older or half-soft in the head or just liked to keep to themselves. Even before that. At home I'd never had friends either. I couldn't afford to, couldn't let them see what my house was like, didn't want anyone paying attention or asking questions.

Alone. I'd been alone my whole life. 'Why did you change your mind?' I said.

He smiled a little. 'Because I knew you thought I'd bail.'

I stared at him. 'You crossed over to the other side – you risked your life – just to prove a point?'

'Not to prove a point,' he said. 'To prove you wrong.' He smiled, bigger this time. His hair smelled like smoke from the fire. 'You seem like you might be worth it.'

Then he kissed me. He leaned over and just touched his lips to mine with Blue held between us like a secret, and I knew then that I would not be so alone anymore.

'How did you—?' Lena is breathless, white in the face. Shock, maybe. Her palms are cut up, and there's blood on her jacket. 'Where did you—?'

'Later,' I say. My cheek is stinging. Got a face full of glass when Lena decided to break through the observation deck, but it's nothing a pair of tweezers can't fix. I'm lucky the glass missed my eyes.

Julian, up close, looks different than he does in all the DFA literature. Younger, and kind of sad and overeager, like a puppy begging for attention – even a swift kick.

Luckily, he asks no questions, just falls in behind me, walking quickly, saying nothing. He must be used to obeying. If it wasn't for Lena, if she hadn't switched up the rules, the needle would be in his arm by now, and he'd be dead. It would have been better for us, and for the movement.

No point in thinking about that now. Lena took a stand, and so I took a stand with her.

That's what you do for family. Anything.

We go out the emergency exit to the fire escape, which leads down into the little courtyard I scouted earlier. So far, so good. Lena's breathing fast and hard behind me, but my breath is easy, even and slow.

This is my favorite part of the story: the escape.

Tack is waiting with the van on Twenty-Fourth Street, just like he said he would be. I open the cargo door and shut Lena and Julian inside.

'Got 'em?' Tack asks when I climb into the passenger seat.

'Would I be here if I hadn't?' I answer.

He frowns. 'You're bleeding.'

I flip down the mirror and take a look: a few uneven cuts on my cheek and neck, beaded with blood. 'Just a scratch,' I say, blotting the blood with the sleeve of my sweatshirt.

'Let's roll, then,' Tack says, and sighs.

He guns the engine and pulls out into the street, gray and blurry with old rain. I keep my sleeve pressed to the side of my face to stanch the bleeding. We make it all the way to the West Side Highway before Tack speaks again.

'It's a risk, taking him back with us,' he says in a low voice. 'Julian Fineman. Shit. A big risk.'

'I'll take responsibility.' I turn my face to the window. I can see the ghost-outlines of my reflection, feel the hum of cold air through the glass.

'She's important to you, isn't she? Lena, I mean.' Tack's voice stays quiet.

'She's important to the movement,' I answer, and see the ghost-girl speak too, her teeth flashing, superimposed over passing images of the city.

Tack doesn't say anything for a second. Then I feel his hand on my knee. 'I would have done it for you, too,' he says, even quieter. 'If you'd been taken. I would have gone back. I would have risked it.'

I turn to look at him. 'You already did come back for me,' I say. I remember that first kiss, and Blue's warmth between us, and Tack's lips, dry as bone, soft as shadow. I still can't say her name, but I think he knows what I'm thinking. 'You came back for us.'

Recently I've been having the fantasy more and more: the one where Tack and I run away, disappear under the wide-open sky into the forest with leaves like green hands, welcoming us. In my fantasy, the more we walk, the cleaner we get, like the woods are rubbing away the past few years, all the blood and the fighting and the scars – sloughing off the bad memories and the false starts, leaving us shiny and new, like dolls just taken out of the package.

And in this fantasy, my fantasy life, we find a stone cottage hidden deep in the forest, untouched, fitted with beds and rugs and plates and everything we need to live – like the owners just picked up and walked away, or like the house had been built for us and was just waiting all this time.

We fish the stream and hunt the woods in the summer. We grow potatoes and peppers and tomatoes big as pumpkins. In the winter we stay inside by the fire while snow falls around us like a blanket, stilling the world, cocooning it in sleep.

We have four kids. Maybe five. The first one is a girl, stupid beautiful, and we call her Blue.

'Where the hell were you?' Pike's in my face as soon as we make it back to the warehouse.

I don't like Pike. He's moody and mean and he thinks he can boss me – and everyone else – around.

I put a hand on his chest, easing him backward. 'Get out of my airspace.'

'I asked you a question.'

'Don't talk to her that way,' Tack jumps in, already wound up, ready to go.

'It's all right.' I'm suddenly too tired to argue. I keep thinking of Lena's last words to me. *The woman who came for me at Salvage . . . That's my mother. Did you know?* Like I *should* have known. Like it's my fault Lena's mom moved on without a *So long, see you later.*

But I know it's deeper than that. I've always thought of Lena as alone, like me. I always saw myself in her a little bit. But she isn't alone. She has a mother, a *free* mother, a fighter. Someone to be proud of. She has family.

I close my eyes and take a deep breath, think of a stone cottage all wrapped in a haze of snow. I open my eyes again.

'We had to take care of something,' Tack is saying.

'But we're all set now,' I say quickly. I glance over at Tack, trying to communicate with my eyes – *let it go, drop it, let's get out of here.*

'We almost left without you,' Pike says, still not ready to forgive us.

'Give us twenty minutes,' I say, and at last Pike shifts aside and lets us pass.

The room where we've been sleeping has been stripped down: cots dismantled, gear packed up. Everyone's getting ready to move on. Once the regulators figure out it was Invalids who sprang Julian – maybe they've already figured it out – they'll do a sweep. They'll come looking up here eventually.

There's no sign of the boy who arrived late last night, the escapee from the Crypts. Young. Quiet type. Barely said a word before falling into bed. He looked like he'd been worked over pretty bad.

He's from Lena's part of the world. I can't help but wonder.

'One of my knives is missing,' Tack says. He peels the mattress of the cot away from the frame. That's where we stash the stuff that matters, the stuff we don't want other people poking at and looking through. It's not exactly a hiding place, since everyone does it – more like a boundary. Tack starts going crazy, pulling off the thin blankets, thumping out the pillows. 'One of my *best* knives.'

For a second, the need to tell is overwhelming. It builds like a bubble in my chest. *Let's go,* I almost say. *Just you and me. Let's leave the fight behind.*

Instead I say, 'How about you check the van.'

When Tack leaves the room, I'm left alone. Suddenly I need to see it again, need to know that it's true. I squat down and stick my hand in the space between my mattress and the cheap metal frame. After a minute of fumbling, I find it: a small meter, barely bigger than a spoon, carefully wrapped in a plastic bag. It cost me one of Tack's best knives and a silver-and-turquoise necklace Lena gave to me when she first crossed over; the trader who agreed to get it for me kept emphasizing the risks. Everyone knows it's impossible to get a pregnancy test nowadays, she was saying. You have to have documentation. Letters of approval from the regulatory board. Blah, blah, blah.

I paid. I had to. I needed to know.

I sit back on my heels and smooth down the thin plastic, so I can read the results: two faint parallel lines, like a ladder leading somewhere.

Pregnant.

Footsteps sound in the hallway. I quickly stuff the test back under the mattress. My heart is beating heavy, quick. Maybe it's my imagination, but I think I feel another heart-beat, a faint pulse somewhere beneath my rib cage, answering.

The first one, we'll name Blue.

# ALEX

L et me tell you something about dying: it's not as bad as they say.

It's the coming-back-to-life part that hurts.

I was a kid again in Rhode Island, running through the gallery, heading toward the ocean.

The gallery was what we called the long, covered walkway that ran from the harbor all the way to the old square, where you could still find bombs, undetonated, embedded in the brick. There was a rumor that went around among us – if you stepped on one, you'd explode. This kid Zero once dared me to do it, and I did just so he'd leave me alone. Nothing happened. Still, I wouldn't have done it again.

You never know. A second time it could go *boom*.

The gallery was all in brick and housed shops that a

hundred years ago must have catered to tourists, vacationers, families. The storefront windows were all gone, maybe shot out, but probably just broken after the blitz, when anyone who survived went looting for supplies. There was, in order: Lick 'n' Swirl Ice Cream; Benjamin's Pizza; the Arcade; the Gift Gallery; T-Shirts-n-More; Franny's Ice Cream. The ice cream machines had been taken apart for scrap, but the pizza oven in Benjamin's was still there, big as a car, and sometimes we used to stick our heads inside and inhale and pretend we smelled baking bread.

There were also two art galleries, and funny enough, most of the art was still hanging on the walls. You can't use paintings as shovels or canvas as a blanket; no point in stealing art, no one to sell it to after the blitz and no money to buy it with. There were photographs of tourists from Before, wearing bright T-shirts and strappy sandals and eating ice cream cones piled high with different-colored scoops, and paintings of the beach at dawn, and at dusk, and at night, and in the rain, and in the snow. There was one painting, I remember, that showed a broad, clean sweep of sky and the ocean drawn out to the horizon, and the sand littered with seashells and crabs and mermaid's purses and bits of seaweed. A boy and girl were standing four feet apart, not facing each other, not acknowledging each other in any way, just standing, looking out at the water.

I always liked that painting. I liked to think they had a secret.

So when I died and turned kid again I went back there, back to the gallery – before Portland, and the move up north, and her. All the stores had been repaired, and there were hundreds of people standing behind the glass, palms pressed to the windowpanes, watching me as I ran. They were all shouting to me, but I couldn't hear them. The glass was too thick. All I could see was the ghost-fog of their breath against the glass and their palms, flat and pale, like dead things.

The longer I ran, the farther the ocean seemed, and the smaller I got, until I was so small I was no bigger than a piece of dust. Until I was no bigger than an idea. I knew I'd be okay if I could only reach the ocean, but the gallery just kept on growing, huge and full of shadows, and all those people kept calling to me silently from behind the glass.

Then a wave came and pushed me backward, and slammed me against something made of stone, and I became big again. My body exploded outward like I'd gone and stepped on that bomb and I was breaking apart into ten thousand pieces.

Everything was on fire. Even my eyes hurt when I tried to open them.

'I don't believe it,' were the first words I heard. 'Someone up there must be looking after him.'

Then someone else: 'No one looks after this garbage.'

I was alive again. I wanted to die.

One time, when I was twelve, I burned down a house.

Nobody was living there. That's why I chose it. It was just some half-run-down white clapboard farmhouse, sitting in the middle of a bunch of lumpy outhouses and barns, like deer turds gathered at the bottom of a big hill. I have no idea what happened to the family that used to live there, but I liked to imagine that they'd gone off to the Wilds, made a clean break for the border once the new regulations kicked in, once people started getting locked up for disagreeing.

It was close to the border, only fifty feet from the fence. That's why I chose it too.

I had started with small things – matchbooks, papers; then piles of leaves, heaped carefully into a garbage can; then a little locked wooden shed on Rosemont Avenue. I watched from Presumpscot Park, sitting on a bench, while the firemen came to put out the shed fire, sirens screaming, geared up. I watched while the neighbors gathered, until there were so many they blocked my view and I tried to stand. But I couldn't stand. My feet and legs were numb. Like bricks. So I just sat and sat, until the crowd thinned and I saw the shed wasn't a shed anymore but just a pile of charred wood and metal and molten plastic, where a bunch of toys had fused together.

All because of the smallest spark. All because of the *click* of a lighter in my hand.

I couldn't stop.

Then: a house. It was summer, six o'clock, dinner hour. I figured if anyone smelled the smoke they might think it was a barbecue, and I'd have plenty of time to get out of there. I used rags stuffed with kerosene and a Bic lighter I had stolen from the desk of the principal's office at my school: yellow with smiley faces on it.

Right away I knew it was a mistake. The house went up in less than a minute. The flames just . . . swallowed it. The smoke blocked out the sun and turned the air blurry from the heat. The smell was awful. Maybe there'd been dead animals in the house, mice and raccoons. I hadn't thought to check.

But the worst was the noise. It was louder, way louder, than I had expected. I could hear wood popping, splitting apart, could hear individual splinters burst and crackle into nothing. Like the house was screaming. But weirdly, when the roof went down, there wasn't any sound at all. Or maybe I couldn't hear by then, because my lungs were full of smoke and my head was pounding and I was running as fast as I could. I called the fire department from an old pay phone, disguising my voice. I didn't stay to watch them come.

They saved the barn, at least. I found out later. I even went to a few parties there, years afterward, on nights I couldn't stand it anymore: all the pretending, the secrets, the sitting around and waiting for instructions.

I even saw her there, once.

But I never went back without remembering the fire – the way it ate up the sky, the sound of a house, a *something*, shriveling into nothing.

That's what it was like waking up in the Crypts. No-longer-dead. But without her.

Like burning alive.


I have nothing to say about my months there. Imagine it, then imagine worse, then give up and know you can't imagine it.

You think you want to know, but you don't.

No one expected me to live, so it was like a game to the guards to see how much I could take. One guy, Roman, was the worst. He was ugly – fat lips, eyes glassed over like a fish on ice in the grocery store – and mean as hell. He liked to put his cigarettes out on my tongue. He cut the insides of my eyelids with razors. Every time I blinked, I felt like my eyes were exploding. I used to lie awake at night and imagine wrapping my hands around his throat, killing him slowly.

See? I told you. You don't want to know.

But the worst was where they put me. The old cell where I'd once stood with Lena, staring at the words etched into the stone. A single word, actually. Just *love*, over and over.

They'd patched up the hole in the wall, reinforced it and barred it with steel. But I could still taste the outside, still smell the rain and hear the distant roar of the river beneath me. I could watch the snow bending whole trees into submission, could lick the icicles that formed on the other side of the bars.

That was torture – being able to see, and smell, and hear, and being trapped in a cage. Like standing on the wrong side of the fence, only a few feet from freedom, and knowing you'll never cross it.

Yeah. Like that.

I got better – somehow, miraculously, without wanting it or willing it or trying. My skin grew together, sealed in the bullet, still lodged somewhere between two ribs. My fever went down, and I stopped seeing things whenever I closed my eyes: people with holes in their faces instead of mouths, buildings catching fire, skies filled with blood and smoke. My heart kept going, and some small, distant part of me was glad.

Slowly, slowly, I grew back into my body. One day, I managed to stand up. A week later, to walk the cell, staggering between the walls like a drunk.

I got a beating for that one – for healing too fast. After that I moved only at night, in the dark, when the guards were too lazy to do random checks, when they slept or drank or played cards instead of making the rounds.

I wasn't thinking of escape. I wasn't thinking of her. That came later. I wasn't thinking anything at all. It was just will, forcing my blood through my veins and my heart to keep opening and shutting and my legs to try and move.

When I remembered, I remembered being a little kid. I thought about the homestead on the Rhode Island coast, long before I moved homesteads with a few others and came to Maine: the gallery and the smell of low tide, and all the brick covered in layers of bird shit, crusty as salt spray. I remembered the boats this guy Flick made out of timber and scrap, and the time he took me fishing and I hooked my first trout: the blush pink of its belly and how good it tasted, like nothing I'd ever eaten before. I remembered Brent, who was my age and like a brother, and how his finger looked after he got cut on an old bit of razor wire, puffy and dark as a storm cloud, and how he screamed when they cut it off to stop the infection from spreading. Dirk and Mel and Toadie: all of them dead, I heard later, killed on some secret mission to Zombieland. And Carr, in Maine, who taught me all about the resistance, who helped me memorize facts about the new me when it was time for me to cross over.

And I remembered my first night in Portland, how I couldn't get comfortable on the bed, and how I moved onto the floor, finally, and fell asleep with my cheek against the rug. How weird everything was: the supermarkets stocked with food I'd never seen before, and trash bins heaped with stuff that was still usable, and rules, rules for everything: eating, sitting, talking, even pissing and wiping yourself.

In my mind, I was reliving my whole life again – slowly, taking my time. Delaying.

Because I knew, sooner or later, I'd get to her.

And then . . . Well, I'd already died once. I couldn't live through it again.

The guards lost interest in me after a while.

In the quiet, and the dark, I got stronger.

Eventually she came. She appeared suddenly, exactly like she'd done that day – she stepped into the sunshine, she jumped, she laughed and threw her head back, so her long ponytail nearly grazed the waistband of her jeans.

After that, I couldn't think about anything else. The mole on the inside of her right elbow, like a dark blot of ink. The way she ripped her nails to shreds when she was nervous. Her eyes, deep as a promise. Her stomach, pale and soft and gorgeous, and the tiny dark cavity of her belly button.

I nearly went crazy. I knew she must think I was dead. What had happened to her after crossing the fence? Had she made it? She had nothing, no tools, no food, no idea where to go. I imagined her weak, and lost. I imagined her dead. She might as well be.

I told myself that if she was alive she would move on, she would forget me, she would be happy again. I tried to tell myself that was what I wanted for her.

I knew I would never see her again.

But hope got in, no matter how hard and fast I tried to stomp it out. Like these tiny fire ants we used to get in Portland. No matter how fast you killed them, there were always more, a steady stream of them, resistant, ever-multiplying.

*Maybe,* the hope said. *Maybe.*

\*     \*     \*

Funny how time heals. Like that bullet in my ribs. It's there, I know it's there, but I can barely feel it at all anymore.

Only when it rains. And sometimes, too, when I remember.

The impossible happened in January, on a night like all other winter nights, frigid, black and long.

The first explosion woke me from a dream. Two other explosions followed, buried somewhere beneath layers of stone, like the rumblings of a faraway train. The alarms started screaming but just as quickly went silent.

The lights shut off all at once.

People were shouting. Footsteps echoed in the halls. The prisoners began banging on walls and doors, and the darkness was full of shouting.

I knew right away it must be freedom fighters. I could *feel* it, the way I could always feel it in my fingertips when I was supposed to do a job, like a drop, and something was wrong – an undercover cop hanging around, or a problem with a contact. Then I'd keep my head down, keep it moving, regroup.

Later I found out that in the lower wards, two hundred cell doors swung open simultaneously. Electrical problem. Two hundred prisoners made a break for it, and a dozen had made it out before the police and regulators showed up and started shooting.

Our doors were closed with deadbolts, and stayed shut.

I beat on the door so hard my knuckles split. I screamed until my voice dried up in my throat. We all did. All of us in Ward Six, all of us forgotten, left to rot. The minutes that had passed since the lights went off felt like hours.

'Let me out!' I screamed, over and over. 'Let me out. I'm one of you.'

And then, a miracle: a small cone of light, a flashlight sweeping down the hall, and the pattern of fast footsteps. I'll admit it. I called to be let out first. I'm not too proud to say it. I'd spent five months in that hellhole, and escape was on the other side of the door. Days, years passed before my door swung open.

But it did. Swing open.

I recognized the guy with the keys. I knew him as Kyle, though I doubt that was his real name. I'd seen him at one or two meetings of the resistance. I'd never liked him. He wore really tight button-down shirts and pants that made him look like he had a constant wedgie.

He wasn't wearing a button-down then. He was wearing all black, and a ski mask pushed back on his head, so I could see his face. And in that moment, I could have kissed him.

'Let's go, let's go.'

It was chaos. It was hell. Emergency lights flashing, illuminating in strobe prisoners clawing at one another to get through the doors, and guards swinging with clubs or firing, randomly, into the crowd to hold them back. Bodies in the halls, and blood smearing the linoleum, speckled on the walls.

I knew from all my times at the Crypts, there was a service entrance in the basement, next to the laundry room. By the time I made it to the first floor, the cops were flowing in, bug-eyed in their riot gear. The screaming was so loud. You couldn't even hear what the cops were yelling. Five feet away from me, I watched some woman wearing a hospital gown and paper slippers shank a cop right in the neck with a pen. I thought, *Good for her*.

Like I said: I'm not too proud.

There was a pop, and a fizz, and something went ricocheting down the hall. Then a hard burn in my eyes and throat and I knew they'd chucked in the tear gas, and if I didn't get out then, I'd never get out. I made for the laundry chute, trying to breathe through the filthy cotton of my sleeve. Pushing people when I had to. Not caring.

You have to understand. I wasn't just thinking of me. I was thinking of her, too.

It was a long shot, but I had no choice. I crawled into the laundry chute, as narrow as a coffin, and dropped. Four long seconds of darkness and free fall. I could hear my breath echoing in the metal cage.

Then I was down. I landed in a big pile of sheets and pillowcases that smelled like sweat and blood and things I didn't want to think about. But I was safe, and nothing was broken. The laundry room was black, empty, the old machines still. The whole room had that moist feel that all laundry rooms do, like a big tongue.

I could still hear screaming and gunshots from upstairs, rolling down the laundry chute, amplified and transformed. It sounded like the world was ending.

But it wasn't.

Out of the laundry room, around the corner, no problem at all. The service door was supposed to be alarmed, but I knew the staff always disabled it so they could go out for smoke breaks without going upstairs.

So: outside, and to the black rush of the Presumpscot River. To freedom.

For me, the world was beginning.

*     *     *

How did I love her?

Let me count the ways.

The freckles on her nose like the shadow of a shadow; the way she chewed on her lower lip when she was thinking and the way her ponytail swung when she walked and how when she ran she looked like she was born going fast and how she fit perfectly against my chest; her smell and the touch of her lips and her skin, which was always warm, and how she smiled. Like she had a secret.

How she always made up words during Scrabble. Hyddym (secret music). Grofp (cafeteria food). Quaw (the sound a baby duck makes). How she burped her way through the alphabet once, and I laughed so hard I spat out soda through my nose.

And how she looked at me like I could save her from everything bad in the world.

This was my secret: she was the one who saved me.

I had trouble finding the old homestead. It took me almost a full day. I'd crossed over the river, into a part of the Wilds I didn't know, and there were no landmarks to guide me. I knew I had to circle southeast, and I did, keeping the city's perimeter in my sights. It was cold outside, but there was lots of sun, and ice ran off the branches. I had no jacket, but I didn't even care.

I was free.

There should have been freedom fighters around, escaped prisoners from the Crypts. But the woods were silent and empty. Sometimes I saw a shape moving through the trees and turned around, only to see a deer bounding away, or a raccoon moving, hunched, through the undergrowth. I found out later that the Incidents in Portland were carried out by a tiny, welltrained group – only six people in total. Of them, four were caught, tried and executed for terrorism.

I found the old homestead at last, long after it got dark, when I was using the moon to navigate and piling up branches as markers so I could be sure I wasn't just turning in circles. I smelled smoke and followed it. I came out into the long alley, where Grandpa Jones and Caitlyn and Carr used to set up shop in their patched-up tents and makeshift houses, where the old trailers stood. It seemed like a lifetime ago I'd lain in bed with Lena and felt her breath tickling my chin and held her while she slept, felt her heart beating through her skin to mine.

It *was* a lifetime ago. Everything was different.

The homestead had been destroyed.

There'd been a fire. That much was obvious. The trees in the surrounding area were bare stumpy fingers, pointing blackly to the sky, as if accusing it of something. It looked like there'd been bombs, too, from the covering of metal and plastic and broken glass vomited across the grass. Only a few trailers were still intact. Their walls were black with smoke; whole walls had collapsed, so charred interiors were visible – lumpy forms that might have been beds, tables.

My old house, where I'd lain with Lena and listened to her breathe and willed the darkness to stay dark forever so we could be there, together, always – that was gone completely. Poof. Just some sheet metal and the concrete rubble of the foundation.

Maybe I should have known. Maybe I should have taken it as a sign.

But I didn't. 'Don't move.'

There was a gun against my back before I knew it. I was strong again, but my reflexes were weak. I hadn't even heard the guy coming.

'I'm a friend,' I said.

'Prove it.'

I pivoted slowly, hands up. A guy was standing there, crazy skinny and crazy tall, like a human grasshopper, with the squinty look of someone who needs glasses but can't get them in the Wilds. His lips were chapped, and he kept licking them. His eyes flicked to the fake procedural scar on my neck.

'Look,' I said, and drew up my sleeve, where they'd tattooed my intake number at the Crypts.

He relaxed then, and lowered the gun. 'Sorry,' he said. 'I thought the others would be back by now. I was worried . . .' Then his eyes lit up, as if he had just registered what he said. 'It worked,' he said. 'It worked. The bombs . . . ?'

'Went off,' I said.

'How many got out?'

I shook my head.

He licked his lips again. 'I'm Rogers,' he said. 'Come on. Sit. I got a fire going.'

He told me about what had happened while I'd been inside: a big sweep on the homesteads, extending from Portland all the way down to Boston and into New Hampshire. There'd been planes, bombs, the works, a big show of military might for the people in Zombieland who'd started to believe that the invalids were real, and out there, and growing.

'What happened to the homesteaders?' I asked. I was thinking of Lena. Of course. I was always thinking of Lena. 'Did they get out?'

'Not everyone.' Rogers was twitchy. Always moving, standing

up and sitting down, tapping his foot. 'A lot of them did, though. At least, that's what I heard. They went south, started doing work for the R down there.'

We talked for hours, Rogers and me. Eventually, others came: prisoners who'd made it across the border into the Wilds, and two of the freedom fighters who'd launched the operation. As the darkness drew tighter they materialized through the trees, drawn to the campfire, appearing suddenly from the shadows, white-faced, as if stepping into this world from another. And they were, in a way.

Kyle, constant-wedgie-boy, never made it back. And then I felt bad, really bad.

I never even thanked him.

We had to move. There would be retribution for what we'd done. There would be air strikes, or attacks from the ground. Rogers told me the Wilds weren't safe anymore, not like they used to be.

We agreed to catch a few hours of sleep and then take off. I suggested south. That's where everyone had gone – that's where Lena, if she had survived, would be. I had no idea where. But I would find her.

We were a small, sad group: a bunch of skinny, dirty convicts, a handful of trained fighters, a woman who'd been on the mental ward and wandered off soon after she joined us. We lost two people, actually. One guy, Greg, had been on Ward Six since he was fifteen years old and had been caught by the police distributing dangerous materials: posters for a free underground concert. He must have been forty by then, skinny as a rail and insect-eyed, with hair growing all the way down his back.

He wanted to know when the guards would come by to

bring us food and water. He wanted to know when we were allowed to bathe, and when we could sleep, and when the lights would come on. In the morning, when I woke up, he was already gone. He must have gone back to the Crypts. He'd gotten used to it there.

Rogers shook us all awake before dawn. We'd made camp in one of the remaining trailers. It was decently sheltered from the wind, even though it was missing one of its walls. For a moment, waking up with a layer of frost crusting the blanket and my clothes, with the smell of the campfire stinging the back of my throat and the birds just starting to sing – I thought I was dreaming.

I'd thought I would never see the sky again. Anything, anything is possible, if you can just see the sky.

The attack came sooner than we were expecting.

It was just after noon when we heard them. I knew right away they were untrained – they were making way too much noise.

'You' – Rogers pointed at me – 'up there.' He jerked his head toward a small embankment; at the top were the ruins of a house. 'Everyone, split. Spread out. Just let 'em pass.' But he shoved a gun in my hand, one of the few we had.

It had been a long time since I'd held a gun. I hoped I'd remember how to shoot.

The leaves crunched under my shoes as I jogged up the hill. It was a clear day, cold, and my breath burned in my lungs. The old house had the rotten smell of an unwashed sock. I pushed open the door and crouched in the dark, leaving the door cracked open an inch so I could keep watch.

'What the hell are you doing?'

The voice made me spin around and nearly topple over. The man was filthy. His hair was long, wild and reached below his shoulders.

'It's all right,' I started to say, trying to calm him down. But he cut me off.

'Get out.' He grabbed my shirt. His fingernails were long and sharp, and he stunk. 'Get out. Do you hear me? This is my place. Get out.'

He was getting louder and louder. And the zombies were close – would be on top of us any second.

'You don't understand,' I tried again. 'You're in danger. We all are.'

But now he was wailing. All his words ran together into a single note. 'Getoutgetoutgetout.'

I shoved him down and tried to get a hand over his mouth, but it was too late. There were voices from outside, the *crackle-crackle* of feet through the dry leaves. While my attention was distracted, he bit down on my hand, hard.

'Getoutgetoutgetout!' He started up his screaming as soon as I drew my hand back. 'Getoutgetoutget—'

He was cut silent only by the first volley of bullets.

I'd rolled off him just in time. I threw myself flat on the ground and covered my head. Soft wood and plaster rained down on me as they emptied twenty rounds into the walls. Then there were other shots, this time farther off. Our group had broken cover.

The door squeaked open. A band of sunlight grew around me. I stayed still, on my stomach, hardly breathing, listening.

'This one's dead.' The floorboards creaked; something skittered in the corner.

'How about the other one?'

'He's not moving.'

Holding my breath, willing my muscles not to move, not to twitch even. If my heart was still beating, I couldn't feel it. Time was slowing down, stretching into long, syrupy seconds.

I'd killed only once in my life, when I was ten years old, just before I moved to Portland. Old Man Hicks, we called him. Sixty years old, the oldest person I knew in the Wilds by far, crippled by arthritis, bedridden, cataracts, full-body pain, day in and day out. He begged us to do it. *When the horse ain't no good, you're doing the horse a favor. Put me down,* he used to say. *For the love of God, put me down.*

They made me do it. So I would know that I could. So I would know I was ready.

'Yup.' The man stopped above me. Toed me with one of his boots, right between the ribs. Then squatted. I felt his fingers on my collar, searching for my neck, for my pulse. 'Looks pretty dead to me, all r—'

I rolled over, hooked an arm around his neck and pulled him down on top of me as the second guy brought his gun up and let two bullets loose. He had good aim. The guy I was using like a shield got hit twice in the chest. For a split second, the shooter hesitated, realizing what he'd done, realizing he'd just emptied a round into his partner's chest, and in that second I rolled the body off me, aimed and pulled the trigger. It didn't take more than a single shot.

*Like riding a bike,* I thought, and had a sudden image of Lena on her bike, skidding down onto the beach, legs out, laughing, while her tires shuddered on the sand. I stood up and searched the men for guns, IDs, money.

People do terrible things, sometimes, for the best reasons.

\*    \*    \*

'What's the worst thing you've ever done?'

We were lying on the blanket in the backyard of 37 Brooks, like we always did that summer. Lena was on her side, cheek resting on her hand, hair loose. Beautiful.

'The worst thing I've ever done . . .' I pretended to think about it. Then I grabbed her by the waist and rolled her on top of me as she shrieked and begged me to stop tickling. 'It's what I'm thinking of doing right now.'

She laughed and pushed herself off me. 'I'm serious,' she said. She kept one hand on my chest. She was wearing a tank top, and I could see one of her bra straps – pale seashell-colored pink. I reached out and ran a finger along her collarbones, my favorite place: like the silhouette of tiny wings.

'You have to answer,' she said. And I almost did. I almost told her then. I wanted her to tell me it was okay, that she still loved me, that she would never leave. But then she leaned down and kissed me and her hair tickled my chest, and when she drew back her eyes were bright and honey-colored. 'I want to know all your deep, dark secrets.'

'All of them? You sure?'

'Mm-hmm.'

'You were in my dream last night.'

Her eyes were smiling. 'Good dream?'

'Come here,' I said. 'I'll show you.' I rolled her down onto the blanket and moved on top of her.

'You're cheating,' she said, but she laughed. Her hair was fanned out across the blanket. 'You didn't answer my question.'

'I don't have to,' I said, and kissed her. 'I'm an angel.'

\*     \*     \*

I'm a liar.

I was lying even then. She deserved an angel, and I wanted to be hers.

When I was in the Crypts, I'd often sat awake and made a list of things she should know, things I would tell her if I ever found her again — like about killing Old Man Hicks when I was ten, how I was shaking so hard Flick had to hold my wrists steady. All the information I passed on when I was in Portland, coded messages and signals — information used I-don't-know-how for I-don't-know-what. Lies I told and had to tell. Times I said I wasn't scared and I was.

And now, these last sins: two regulators, dead.

And one more for the road.

Because when the fight was over, and I came down from the house to take stock of the damage, I saw someone familiar: Roman, the guard from the Crypts, lying in the leaves with a handle sticking out of his chest, his shirt clotted with blood. But alive. His breath was a liquid gargle in his throat.

'Help me,' he said, choking on the words. His eyes were rolling up to the sky, wild, like a horse's. And I remembered Old Man Hicks saying, *When the horse ain't no good, you're doing the horse a favor.*

So I did. Help him. He was dying anyway, slowly. I put a bullet through his head, so it would go quick.

*I'm sorry, Lena.*

We lost three of our group in the fight that day, but the rest of us moved on. We went slowly, zigzagging. Any time we heard rumors of a populated homestead, we scouted for it. Rogers liked the company, the information, the opportunity to communicate with other freedom fighters, restock our

weapons, trade for better provisions. I only cared about one
thing. Each time we got close to a camp, I got my hopes up
all over again. Maybe this one . . . maybe this time . . .
maybe she'd be there. But the farther we got from Portland,
the more I worried. I had no way of finding Lena. No way
of knowing whether she was alive, even.

By the time we made it to Connecticut, spring was coming.
The woods were shaking off the freeze. The ice on the rivers
opened up. There were plants poking up everywhere. We
had good luck. The weather held, we got lucky with a few
rabbits and geese. There was food enough.

Finally, I got a break. We were camping for a few days in
the old husk of a shopping center, all blown-out windows
and low cement buildings with faded signs for hardware and
deli sandwiches and princess nails, a place that kind of
reminded me of the gallery, and we came across a trader who
was going in the opposite direction, heading north to Canada.
He camped with us for the night, and in the evening he
unrolled a thick mohair blanket and spread out all his wares,
whatever he had for sale: coffee, tobacco and rolling papers,
tweezers, antibiotics, sewing needles and pins, a few pairs
of glasses. (Even though none of the glasses in the trader's
collection were the right fit, Rogers traded a knife for a pair
anyway. They were better than nothing.)

Then I saw it: buried in a tangle of miscellaneous jewelry,
crap no one would use except for scrap metal, was a small
turquoise ring on a silver chain. I recognized it immediately.
I'd seen her wear it a hundred times. I'd removed it so I
could kiss her neck, her collarbones. I'd helped her fasten
the little clasp, and she'd laughed because my fingers were
so clumsy.

I reached for it slowly, like it was alive – like it might leap away from my fingers.

'Where did you get this?' I asked him, trying to keep my voice steady. The turquoise felt warm in my hand, as if it still carried a little bit of her heat in the stone.

'Pretty, isn't it?' He was good at what he did: a fast talker, a guy who knew how to survive. 'Sterling and turquoise. Probably sell for a decent amount on the other side. Forty, fifty bucks if you need some quick cash. What are you giving for it?'

'I'm not buying,' I said, though I wanted to. 'I just want to know where you got it.'

'I didn't steal it,' he said.

'Where?' I said again.

'A girl gave it to me,' he said, and I stopped breathing.

'What did she look like?' Big eyes, like maple syrup. Soft brown hair. Perfect.

'Black hair,' he said. No. Wrong. 'Probably early twenties. Had a funny name – Bird. No, Raven. She was from up this way, actually. Came south last year with a whole crew.' He lowered his voice and winked. 'Traded the necklace and a good knife, just for a Test. You know what I mean.'

But I'd stopped listening. I didn't care about the girl, Raven, or whatever her name was – I knew she might have taken it off Lena. I knew this might mean that Lena was dead. But it could mean that she had made it, joined up with a group of homesteaders, made it south. Maybe Lena had traded with the girl, Raven, for something she needed.

It was my only hope.

'Where was she?' I stood up. It was dark already, but I couldn't wait. It was my first – my only – clue about where Lena might be.

'Big warehouse just outside of White Plains,' he said. 'There was a whole big group of 'em. Two or three dozen.' He frowned. 'You sure you don't want to buy it?'

I was still holding on to the necklace. 'I'm sure,' I said. I put it down carefully; I didn't want to leave it behind, but I had nothing but the gun Rogers had given me and a knife I'd taken off one of the regulators, plus a few IDs. Nothing I could trade.

Rogers figured we'd made it ten miles west of Bristol, Connecticut; that meant, roughly figuring, New York City was another one hundred miles and White Plains thirty less than that. I could do thirty miles a day if the terrain was good and I didn't make camp for more than a few hours each night.

I had to try. I had no idea whether Raven was on the move and whether Lena, if she was with them, would soon be moving too. I'd been asking, praying, for a way to find her, for a sign that she was still alive – and a sign had come.

That's the thing about faith. It works.

Rogers gave me a pack with a flashlight, a tarp for bedding down and as much food as he could spare, even though he said it was craziness starting out right away, in the dark, all alone. And he was right. It was craziness. *Amor deliria nervosa.* The deadliest of all deadly things.

Sometimes I think maybe they were right all along, the people on the other side in Zombieland. Maybe it would be better if we didn't love. If we didn't lose, either. If we didn't get our hearts stomped on, shattered; if we didn't have to patch and repatch until we're like Frankenstein monsters, all sewn together and bound up by who knows what.

If we could just float along, like snow.

That's what Zombieland is: frozen, calm, quiet. It's the world after a blizzard, the peacefulness that comes with it, the muffled silence and the sense that nothing in the world is moving. It's beautiful, in its own way.

Maybe we'd be better off.

But how could anyone who's ever seen a summer – big explosions of green and skies lit up electric with splashy sunsets, a riot of flowers and wind that smells like honey – pick the snow?

TURN THE PAGE FOR ONE OF FIVE EXCLUSIVE
EXCERPTS FROM

# REPLICA

## LAUREN OLIVER

You can find them all in

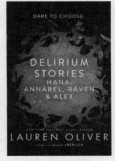

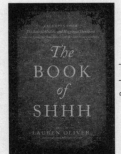

# LYRA

**CHAPTER FOUR**

Cog testing took place in a large, drafty room of D-Wing that had once been used to house cages full of rabbits and still smelled faintly of pellet food and animal urine. Lyra didn't know what had happened to the rabbits. Haven was large, and many of its rooms were off-limits, so she assumed they had been moved. Or maybe they had *failed to thrive*, too, like so many of the replicas.

Every week Cog Testing varied: the replicas might be asked to pick up small and slippery pins as quickly as possible, or attempt to assemble a three-dimensional puzzle, or to pick out visual patterns on a piece of paper. The female replicas, all nine hundred and sixty of them, were admitted by color in groups of forty over the course of the day. Lilac Springs was out of the Box and took the seat next to Lyra's. Lilac Springs had named herself after a product she'd seen advertised on the nurses' TV. Even after the nurses had laughed hysterically and explained to her – and everyone – what a feminine douche was and what it was for, she had refused to change her name, saying she liked the sound of it.

'You don't look so good,' was the first thing Lilac Springs said to Lyra. Lilac Springs hardly ever said anything. She was one of the slower replicas. She still needed help getting dressed, and she had never learned her alphabet. 'Are you sick?'

Lyra shook her head, keeping her eyes on the table. She'd thrown up again in the middle of the night and was so dizzy afterward that she had to stay there, holding on to the toilet, for a good twenty minutes. Cassiopeia had caught her when she came in to pee. But she didn't think Cassiopeia would tell. Cassiopeia was always getting in trouble – for not eating her dinner, for talking, for openly staring at the males and even for trying to talk to them, on the few occasions they wound up in the halls or the Box or the Stew Pot together.

'*I'm sick,*' Lilac Springs said. She was speaking so loudly, Lyra instinctively looked up at the Glass Eyes, even though she knew they didn't register sound. 'They put me in the Box.'

Lyra didn't have friends at Haven. She didn't know what a friend was. But she thought she would be unhappy if Lilac Springs died. Lyra had been five years old when Lilac Springs was made, and could still remember how after Lilac Springs had been birthed and transferred to Postnatal for observation she had kicked her small pink feet and waved her fists as if she was dancing.

But it wasn't looking good. Something was going around the Browns, and the doctors in the Box couldn't stop it. In the past four months, five of them had died – four females, and number 312 from the males' side. Two of them had died the same night. The nurses had suited up in heavy gloves and masks and bundled the bodies in a single plastic tarp before hauling them out for collection. And Lilac Springs's skin was still shiny red and raw-looking, like the skin on top of a blister. Her hair, which was buzzed short like all the other replicas', was patchy. Some of her scalp showed through.

'It's not so bad,' Lilac Springs said, even though Lyra still hadn't responded. 'Palmolive came.'

Palmolive was also a Brown. She had started throwing up a few weeks ago and was found wandering the halls in the middle of the night. She had been transferred to the Box when she could hardly choke down a few sips of water without bringing it up again.

'Do you think I'll be dead soon?' Lilac Springs asked. Fortunately, the nurses came in before Lyra had to answer. Lazy Ass and Go Figure were administering. They almost always did. But earlier, Lyra had been afraid that it might be somebody else.

Today there were three tests. Whenever Lyra's heart beat faster, she imagined its four valves opening and closing like shutters, the flow of blood in one direction, an endless loop like all the interlocking wings of Haven. She had learned about hearts like she'd learned about the rest of the human body: because there was nothing else to learn, no truth at Haven except for the physical, nothing besides pain and response, symptom and treatment, breathe in and breathe out and skin stretched over muscle over bone.

First, Nurse Go Figure called out a series of five letters and asked that the replicas memorize them. Then they had to re-arrange colored slips of paper until they formed a progression, from green to yellow. Then they had to fit small wooden pieces in similarly shaped holes, a ridiculously easy test, although Lilac Springs seemed to be struggling with it – trying to fit the diamond shape into the triangular hole, and periodically drop-ping pieces so they landed, clatteringly, to the floor.

For the last test, Go Figure distributed papers and pens – Lyra held the pen up to her tongue surreptitiously, enjoying the taste of the ink; she wanted another pen badly for her collection – and asked that the replicas write down the five letters they'd memorized, in order. Most of the replicas had learned their numbers to one hundred and the alphabet A through Z, both so they could identify their individual beds and for use in testing, and Lyra took great pleasure in drawing the curves and angles of each number in turn, imagining that numbers, too, were like a language. When she looked up, she saw that Lilac Springs's paper was still completely blank. Lilac Springs was holding her pen clumsily, staring at it as though she'd never seen one. She hadn't even remembered a single number, although Lyra knew she knew her letters and was very proud of it.

Then Lazy Ass called time, and Nurse Go Figure collected the papers, and they sat in silence as the results were collected, tabulated and marked in their files. Lyra's palms began to sweat. Now.

'I forgot the numbers,' Lilac Springs said. 'I couldn't remember the numbers.'

'All right, that's it.' Lazy Ass hauled herself out of her chair, wincing, as she always did after testing. The replicas stood too. Only Lyra remained sitting, her heart clenching and unclenching in her chest.

As always, as soon as Lazy Ass was on her feet, she started complaining: 'Goddamn shoes. Goddamn weather. And now my lazy ass gotta go all the way to Admin. Take me twenty minutes just to get there and back. And those men coming today.' Lazy Ass normally worked the security desk and subbed in to help with testing when she had to. She was at least one hundred pounds overweight, and her ankles swelled in the heat until they were thick and round as the trunks of the palms that lined the garden courtyard.

'Go figure,' said Go Figure, like she always did. She had burnished brown skin that always looked as if it had been recently oiled.

*Now.* Most of the other replicas had left. Only Lilac Springs remained, still seated, staring at the table.

'I'll do it,' Lyra said. She felt breathless even though she hadn't moved, and she wondered whether Lazy Ass would notice. But no. Of course she wouldn't. Many of the nurses couldn't even tell the replicas apart. When she was a kid, Lyra remembered staring at the nurses, willing them to stare back at her, to see her, to take her hand or pick her up or tell her she was pretty. She had once been moved to solitary for two days after she stole Nurse Em's security badge, thinking that the nurse wouldn't be able to leave at the end of the day, that she would *have* to stay. But Nurse Em had found a way to leave, of course, and soon afterward she had left Haven forever.

Lyra had gotten used to it: to all the leaving, to being left. Now she was glad to be invisible. They were invisible to her, too, in a way. That was why she'd given them nicknames.

# GEMMA

**CHAPTER THREE**

Still, she felt the sudden, overwhelming desire to scream. Chloe and her little pack of wolverines had been doing their best to make Gemma miserable for years. But they had never done anything this bad. They'd come to her house. They'd taken the time to fill a Halloween mask with rocks or concrete rubble or metal shrapnel from their mechanical hearts. They had said that she deserved to die. Why? What had she ever done to them?

She was an alien, adrift on an unfriendly planet. Hopeless and lost.

'Are you sure?' Kristina said, smoothing Gemma's face with a thumb. Gemma was scowling.

She took a step backward. 'Positive,' she said.

'Okay.' Kristina exhaled a big breath and gave Finke a weak smile. 'Sorry for all the trouble. You know how girls are.'

'Mm-hmm,' he said, in a tone that he made it clear he didn't and had no desire to, either.

Gemma felt like going straight to her room, possibly forever, but Kristina managed to get an arm around her shoulders. For a thin woman, she was surprisingly strong, and she held Gemma there in a death grip.

'I'm sorry, honey,' she said. 'Why didn't you tell me you were having problems at school?'

She shrugged. 'It's no big deal.'

Kristina smelled, as always, like rose water and very expensive perfume. So expensive that it actually smelled like new-printed money. 'I don't want your father to worry, do you?' She smiled, but Gemma read anxiety in her mother's eyes, decoded the words her mother would never say: *I don't want him to think you're more of a disappointment than he already does.* 'Let's just tell him there was an accident. A kid and a baseball. Something like that.'

To hit a baseball from the street through the living room window, the kid would have to be a first-draft pick for the major leagues. Usually her parents' willingness to lie about things big and small bothered Gemma. If her parents were so good at making up stories, how could she ever be sure they were telling the truth?

Today, however, she could only be grateful.

'Baseball,' she said. 'Sure.'

Gemma woke up in the middle of the night from a nightmare that, thankfully, released her almost as soon as she opened her eyes, leaving only the vague impression of rough hands and the taste of metal. In the hall, Rufus was whimpering.

'What's the matter?' she said, easing out of bed to open the door for him. As soon as she did, she heard it: the sudden swell of overlapping voices, the angry punctuation of silence. Her parents were fighting.

'It's okay, boy,' she whispered to Rufus, threading a hand through the scruff of fur on his neck. He was a baby about fights. Immediately, he darted past her and leapt onto the bed, burying his head in her heap of pillows, as if to block out the sound from downstairs.

She would have gone back to bed, but at exactly that moment, her father's voice crested, and she very clearly heard him say, '*Frankenstein*. For Christ's sake. Why didn't you tell me?'

Gemma eased out into the hall, grateful for the plush rug that absorbed the sound of her footsteps. Quickly, she moved past paneled squares of moonlight, past guest rooms always empty of guests and marble-tiled bathrooms no one ever used, until she reached the main staircase. Downstairs, a rectangle of light yawned across the hallway. Her father's study door was open, and Gemma got a shock. Her mother was perched on the leather ottoman, her face pale and exhausted-looking, her arms crossed at the waist to keep her bathrobe closed. Gemma had never, ever seen anyone besides her father in the study. She had always assumed no one else was allowed to enter.

'I tried calling . . .' Her mother's voice was weak and a little bit slurry, as if all of the edges were lopped off. It must be after midnight. He must have woken her up from a sleeping-pill slumber.

'Feeding me some bullshit story. I had to hear it from Frank at the department. Thank God *someone* respects me.'

Gemma's heart sank. It had been stupid to believe that they could conceal the truth from her father. He had contacts everywhere – in the police department and even in the government, although he kept his most important contacts secret. He'd cofounded the sixth-largest pharmaceutical company in the country, Fine & Ives, which made everything from shampoo to heart medication to drugs for soldiers suffering from PTSD. Although he'd been kicked off the board of his own company after a brutal three-year legal battle when Gemma was a toddler – Gemma had never found out the details, but she knew her dad had disapproved of where the company was putting its resources – he still traveled with a personal security guard and went to Washington, DC, every quarter to meet with politicians and lobbyists and top brass.

Often Gemma feared she would never, ever get truly away from her parents – not even when she went to college, not even when she moved out and moved as far away from Chapel Hill as possible and had her own family. They would always be able to find her. They would always be able to *see* her, wherever she was.

'I respect you,' Kristina protested, and Gemma got a sudden strangled feeling, as if a hand were closing around her throat. Her father was twelve years older than Kristina. He and his twin brother, Ted, had both been to West Point, like their father before them. Geoffrey had gone on to become a military strategist, and he never let anyone – least of all Gemma and her mom – forget it. *Respect*. That was the drumbeat of their lives. *Respect*. He could write a book, she thought, about respect, and discipline, and order, and work. He could probably write a whole series.

On the other hand, what he knew about *acceptance* and *tolerance* and his *own daughter* would barely fill up a tweet.

Sometimes Gemma wondered how it was possible they were made from the same genetic material. Her father was angular and cold everywhere she was warm and soft and sensitive. But the proof was there. She would have so much rather looked like her mother. Instead she had her father's hazel eyes, his square chin, his way of smiling with the corners of his mouth turned down, as if neither of them had ever quite learned to do it correctly.

'I didn't want to worry you,' Gemma's mom went on. 'Gemma said it was just a prank. Some girls have been giving her a hard time at school, and—'

'A prank, Kristina? Are you blind? This wasn't a prank. This was a message. Do you know who Frankenstein is?'

'Of course I know—'

'Frankenstein is the *doctor*. In the original story, in the real version, he's the one who made the monster.' There was a long moment of silence. Gemma could feel her heart beating painfully, swollen like a bruise. 'This was a message for me.'

*He's the one who made the monster.*

*This was a message for me.*

LOOK OUT FOR *THE BOOK OF SHHH*
*AND THE NEXT SNEAK PEEK AT*

# REPLICA

LAUREN
OLIVER